# I KILLED
# ADOLF
# HITLER

by JASON

Colored by HUBERT
FANTAGRAPHICS BOOKS

OTHER BOOKS BY JASON:

*Hey, Wait…*
*Sshhhh!*
*The Iron Wagon*
*Tell Me Something*
*You Can't Get There From Here*
*Why Are You Doing This?*
*Meow, Baby!*
*The Left Bank Gang*
*The Living and the Dead*
*The Last Musketeer* (SPRING 2008)

FANTAGRAPHICS BOOKS
7563 Lake City Way NE
Seattle WA 98115

Designed by Jason and Covey
Production by Jacob Covey
Lettered by Paul Baresh
Edited and translated by Kim Thompson
Published by Gary Groth and Kim Thompson

Special thanks to Jérôme at Editions de Tournon – Carabas.

Distributed in the U.S. by W.W. Norton and Company, Inc. (212-354-5500).
Distributed in Canada by Raincoast Books (800-663-5714).
Distributed in the United Kingdom by Turnaround Distribution (208-829-3009).

Visit the website for Jippi, who originally publishes Jason's work, at www.jippicomics.com.
Visit the website for The Beguiling, where Jason's original artwork can be purchased: www.beguiling.com.
Visit the Fantagraphics website, just because: www.fantagraphics.com.

First printing: June 2007. ISBN: 9878-1-56097-828-2. Printed in Singapore.

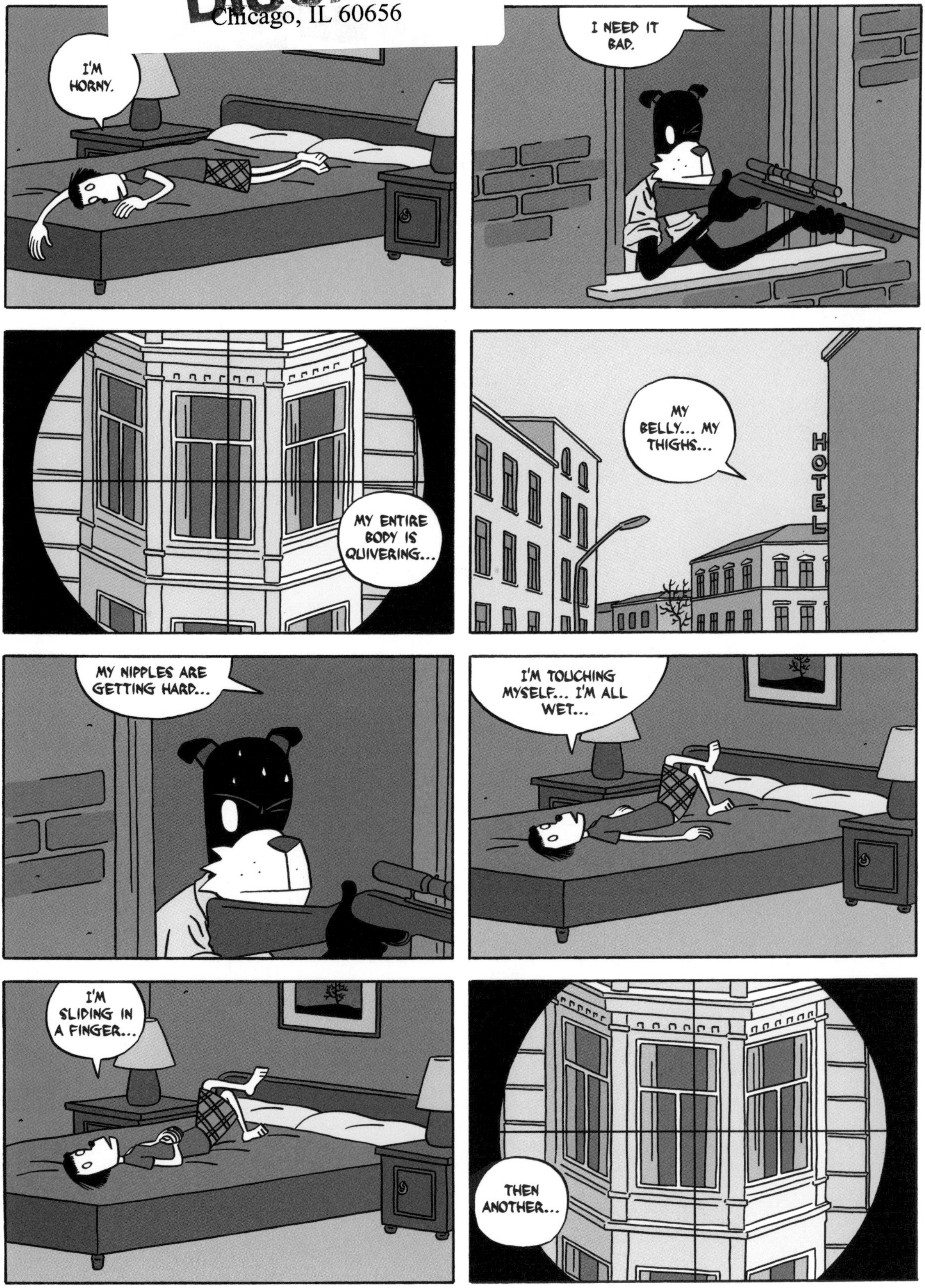
I'M HORNY.
I NEED IT BAD.
MY ENTIRE BODY IS QUIVERING...
MY BELLY... MY THIGHS...
HOTEL
MY NIPPLES ARE GETTING HARD...
I'M TOUCHING MYSELF... I'M ALL WET...
I'M SLIDING IN A FINGER...
THEN ANOTHER...

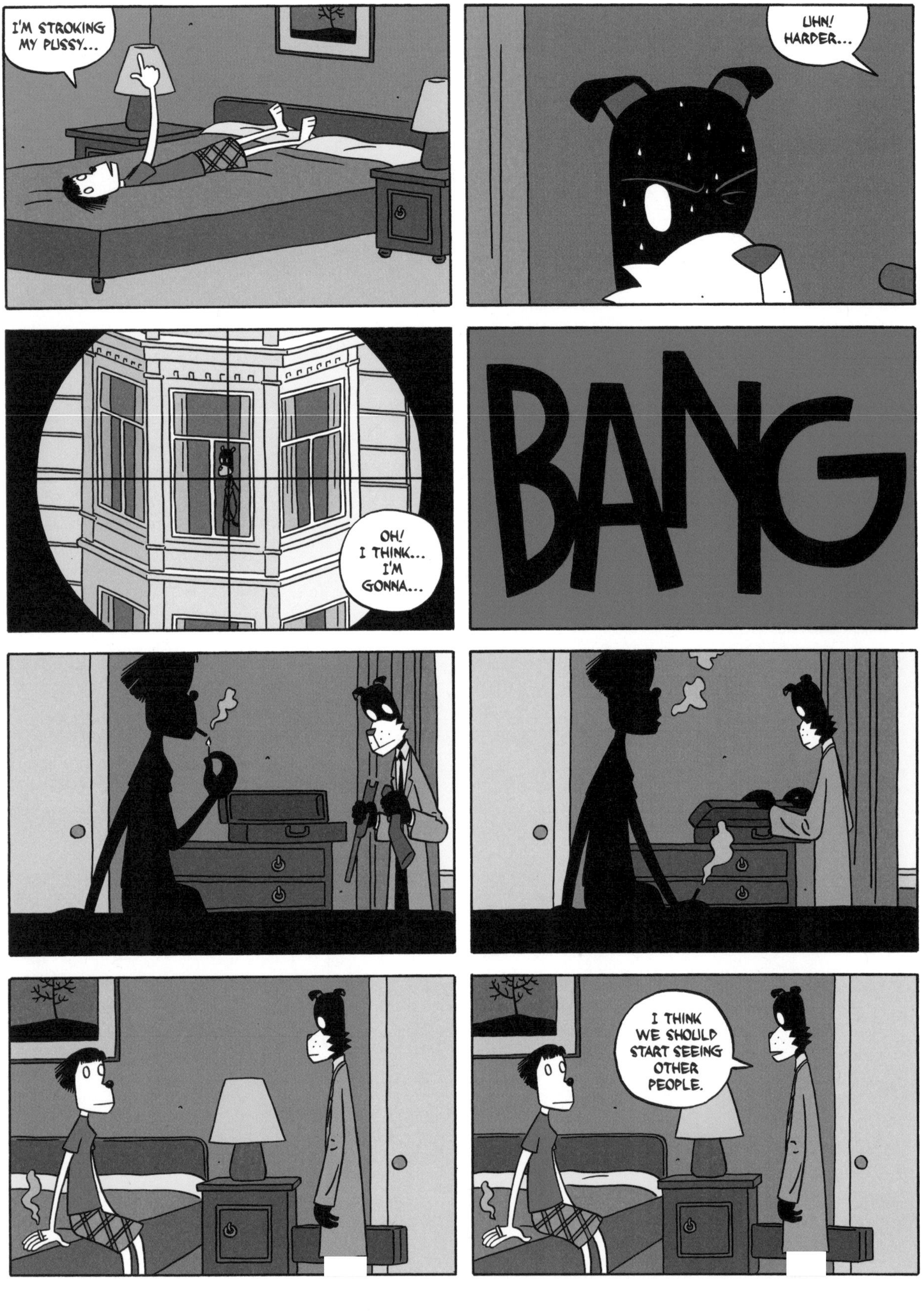
I'M STROKING MY PUSSY...
UHN! HARDER...
OH! I THINK... I'M GONNA...
BANG
I THINK WE SHOULD START SEEING OTHER PEOPLE.

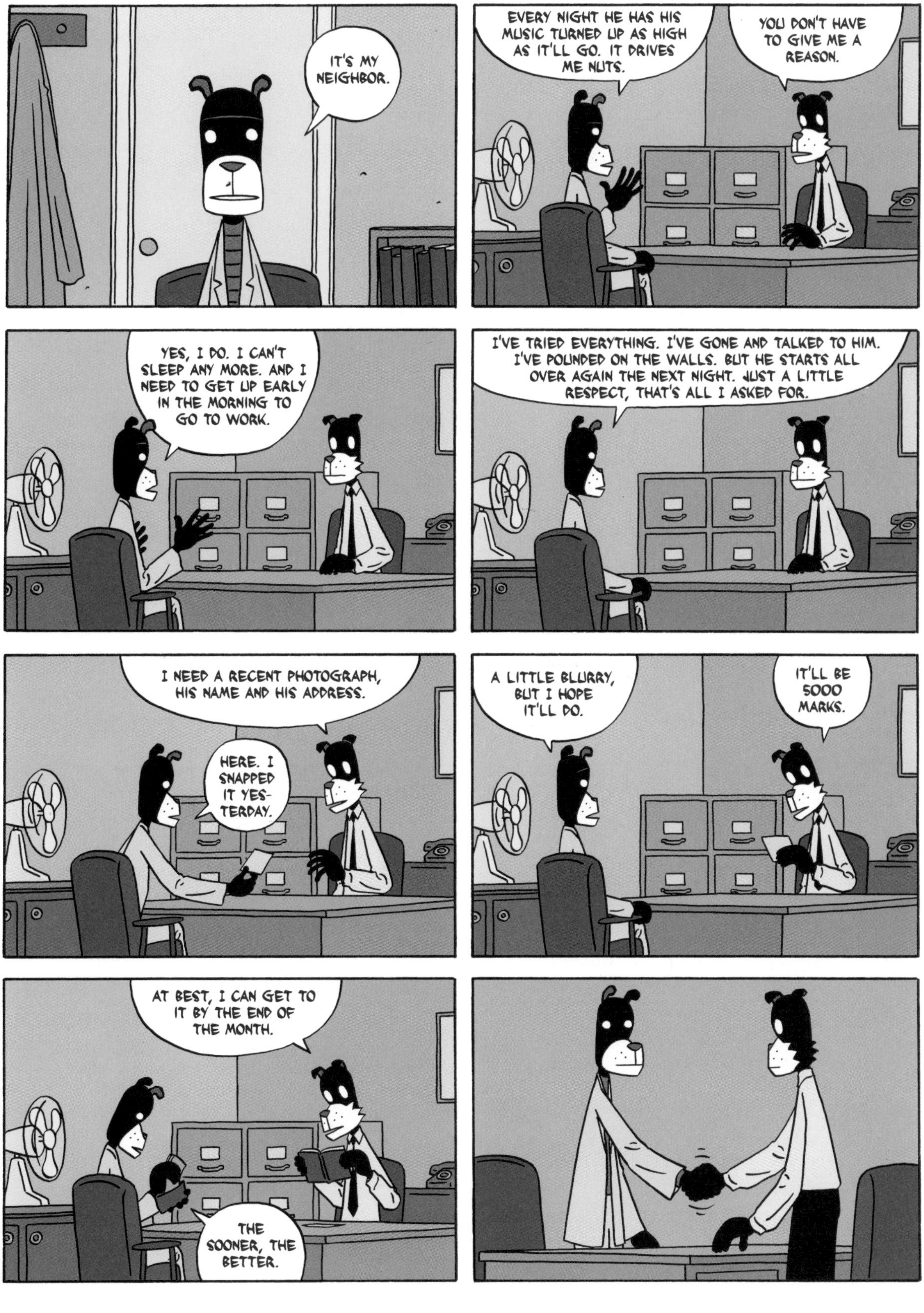
IT'S MY NEIGHBOR.
EVERY NIGHT HE HAS HIS MUSIC TURNED UP AS HIGH AS IT'LL GO. IT DRIVES ME NUTS.
YOU DON'T HAVE TO GIVE ME A REASON.
YES, I DO. I CAN'T SLEEP ANY MORE. AND I NEED TO GET UP EARLY IN THE MORNING TO GO TO WORK.
I'VE TRIED EVERYTHING. I'VE GONE AND TALKED TO HIM. I'VE POUNDED ON THE WALLS. BUT HE STARTS ALL OVER AGAIN THE NEXT NIGHT. JUST A LITTLE RESPECT, THAT'S ALL I ASKED FOR.
I NEED A RECENT PHOTOGRAPH, HIS NAME AND HIS ADDRESS.
HERE. I SNAPPED IT YES-TERDAY.
A LITTLE BLURRY, BUT I HOPE IT'LL DO.
IT'LL BE 5000 MARKS.
AT BEST, I CAN GET TO IT BY THE END OF THE MONTH.
THE SOONER, THE BETTER.

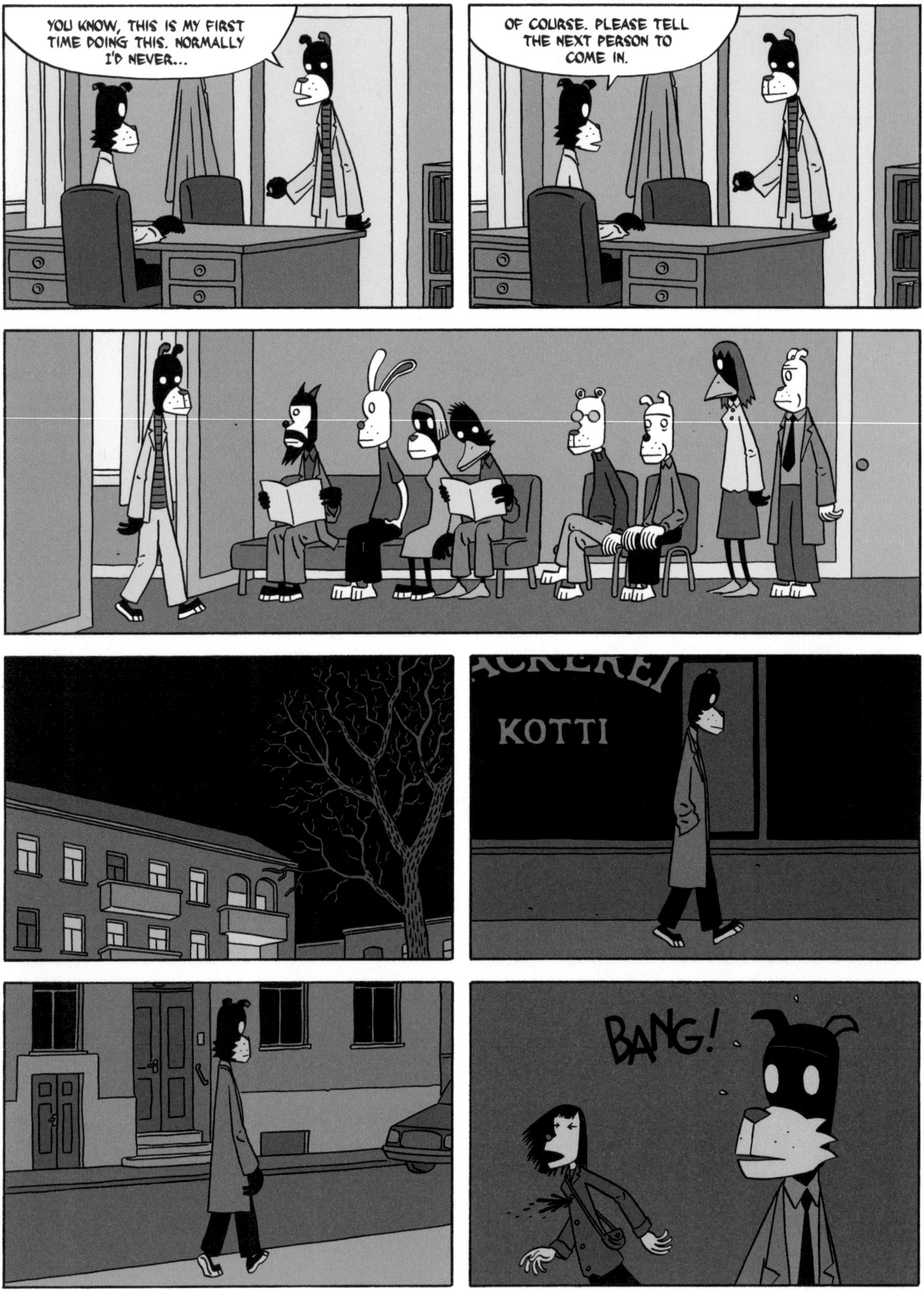
YOU KNOW, THIS IS MY FIRST TIME DOING THIS. NORMALLY I'D NEVER...
OF COURSE. PLEASE TELL THE NEXT PERSON TO COME IN.
ACKEREI
KOTTI
BANG!

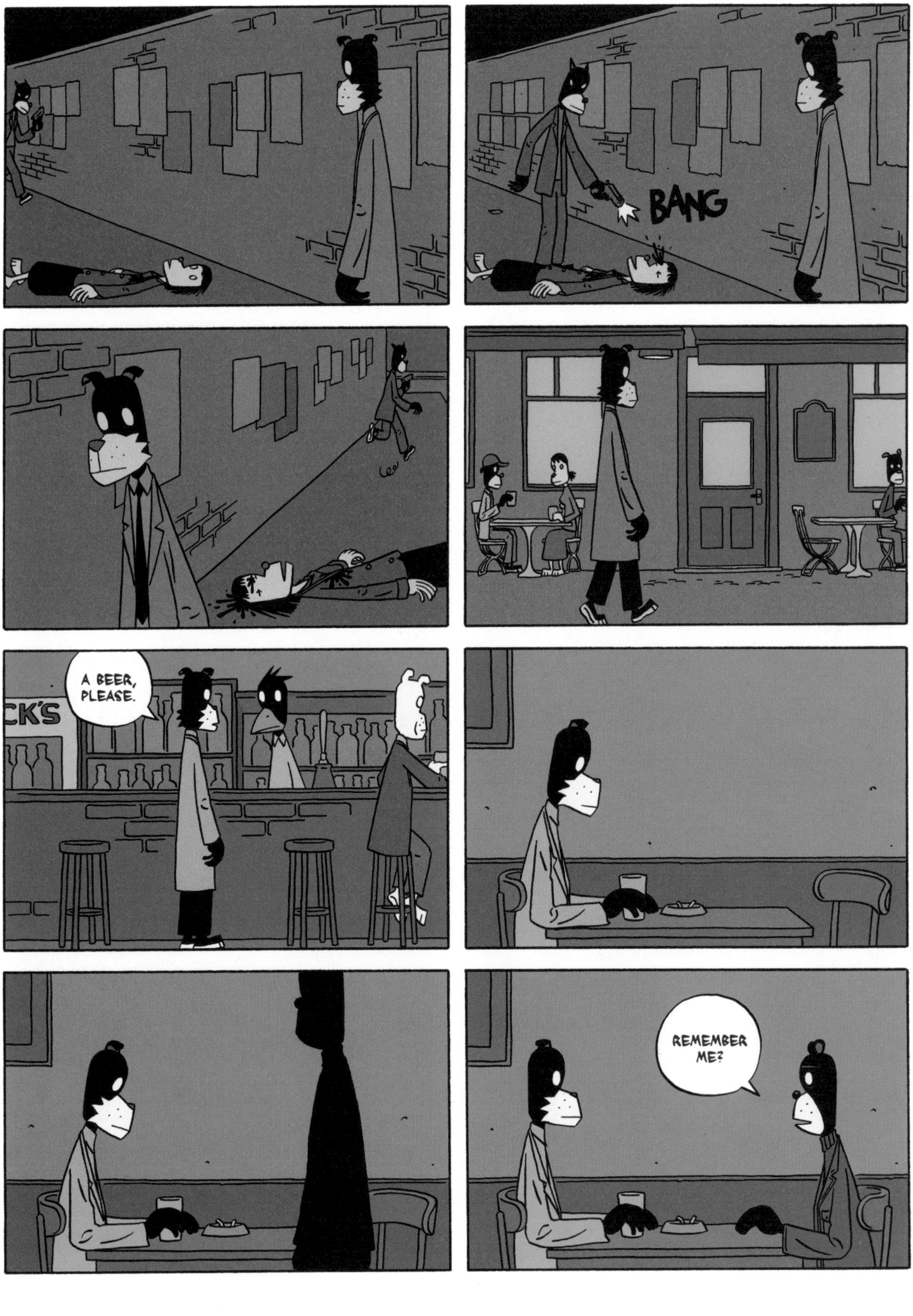
BANG
A BEER, PLEASE.
CK'S
REMEMBER ME?

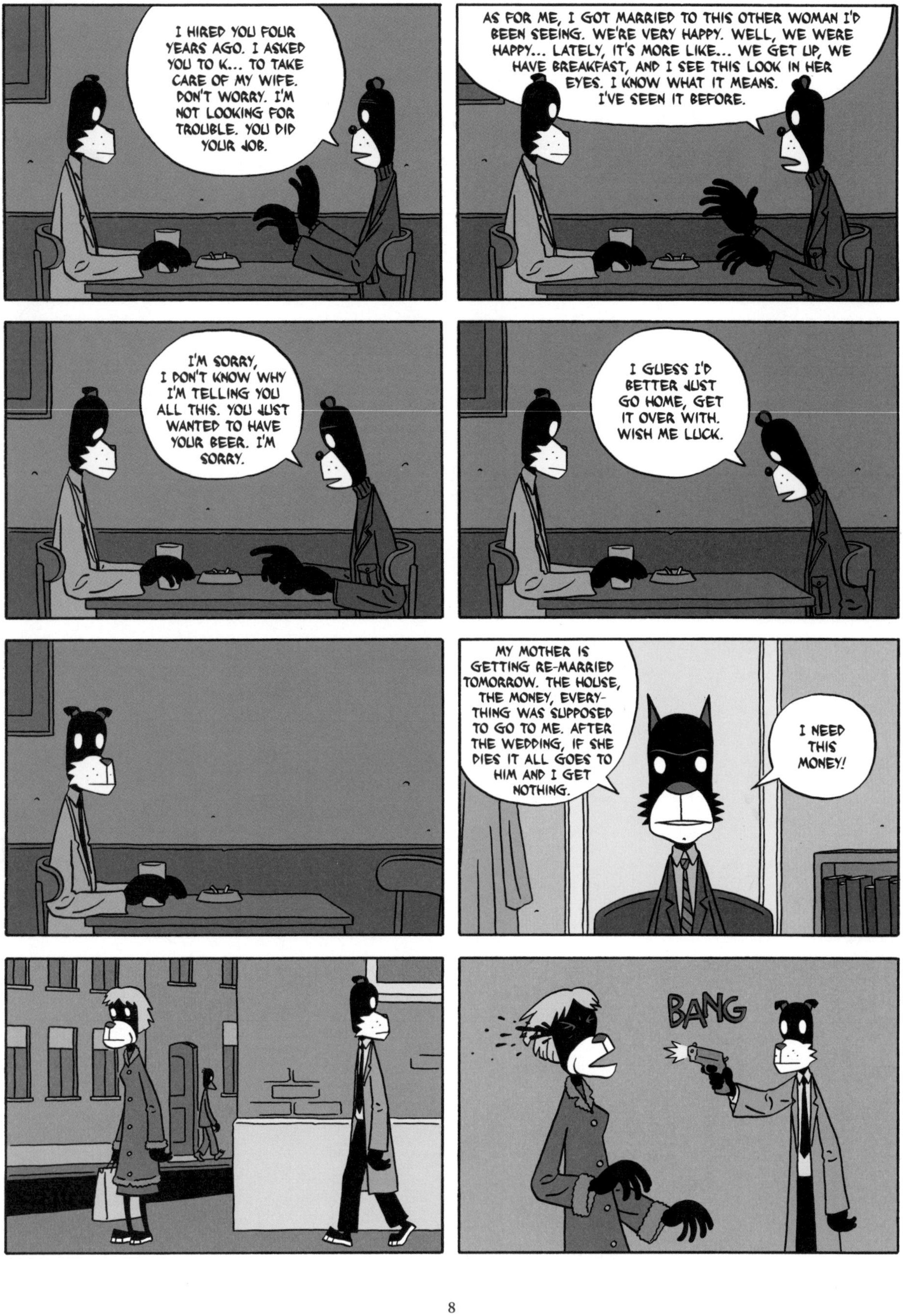
I HIRED YOU FOUR YEARS AGO. I ASKED YOU TO K... TO TAKE CARE OF MY WIFE. DON'T WORRY. I'M NOT LOOKING FOR TROUBLE. YOU DID YOUR JOB.
AS FOR ME, I GOT MARRIED TO THIS OTHER WOMAN I'D BEEN SEEING. WE'RE VERY HAPPY. WELL, WE WERE HAPPY... LATELY, IT'S MORE LIKE... WE GET UP, WE HAVE BREAKFAST, AND I SEE THIS LOOK IN HER EYES. I KNOW WHAT IT MEANS. I'VE SEEN IT BEFORE.
I'M SORRY, I DON'T KNOW WHY I'M TELLING YOU ALL THIS. YOU JUST WANTED TO HAVE YOUR BEER. I'M SORRY.
I GUESS I'D BETTER JUST GO HOME, GET IT OVER WITH. WISH ME LUCK.
MY MOTHER IS GETTING RE-MARRIED TOMORROW. THE HOUSE, THE MONEY, EVERY-THING WAS SUPPOSED TO GO TO ME. AFTER THE WEDDING, IF SHE DIES IT ALL GOES TO HIM AND I GET NOTHING.
I NEED THIS MONEY!
BANG

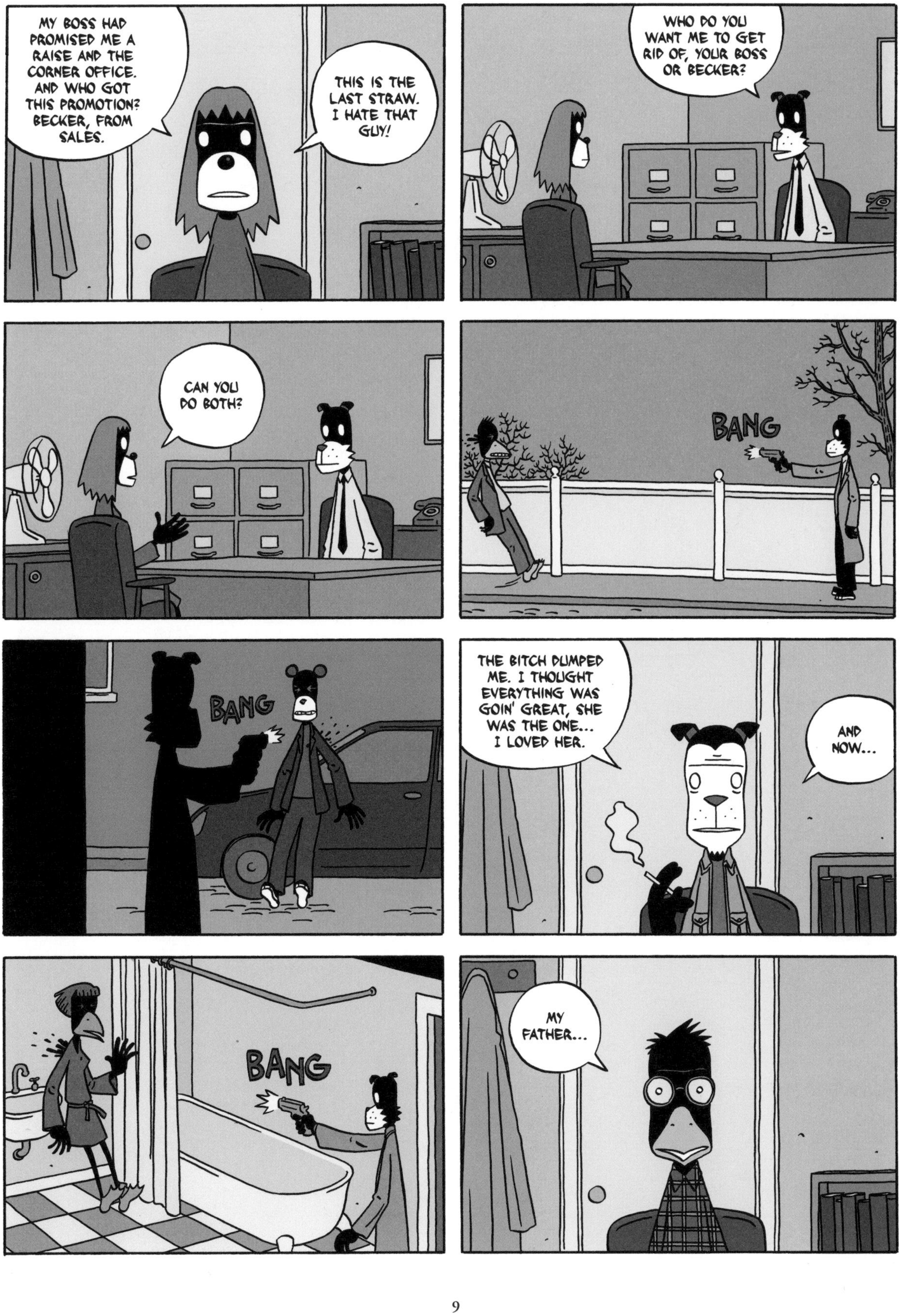
MY BOSS HAD PROMISED ME A RAISE AND THE CORNER OFFICE. AND WHO GOT THIS PROMOTION? BECKER, FROM SALES.
THIS IS THE LAST STRAW. I HATE THAT GUY!
WHO DO YOU WANT ME TO GET RID OF, YOUR BOSS OR BECKER?
CAN YOU DO BOTH?
BANG
BANG
THE BITCH DUMPED ME. I THOUGHT EVERYTHING WAS GOIN' GREAT, SHE WAS THE ONE... I LOVED HER.
AND NOW...
BANG
MY FATHER...

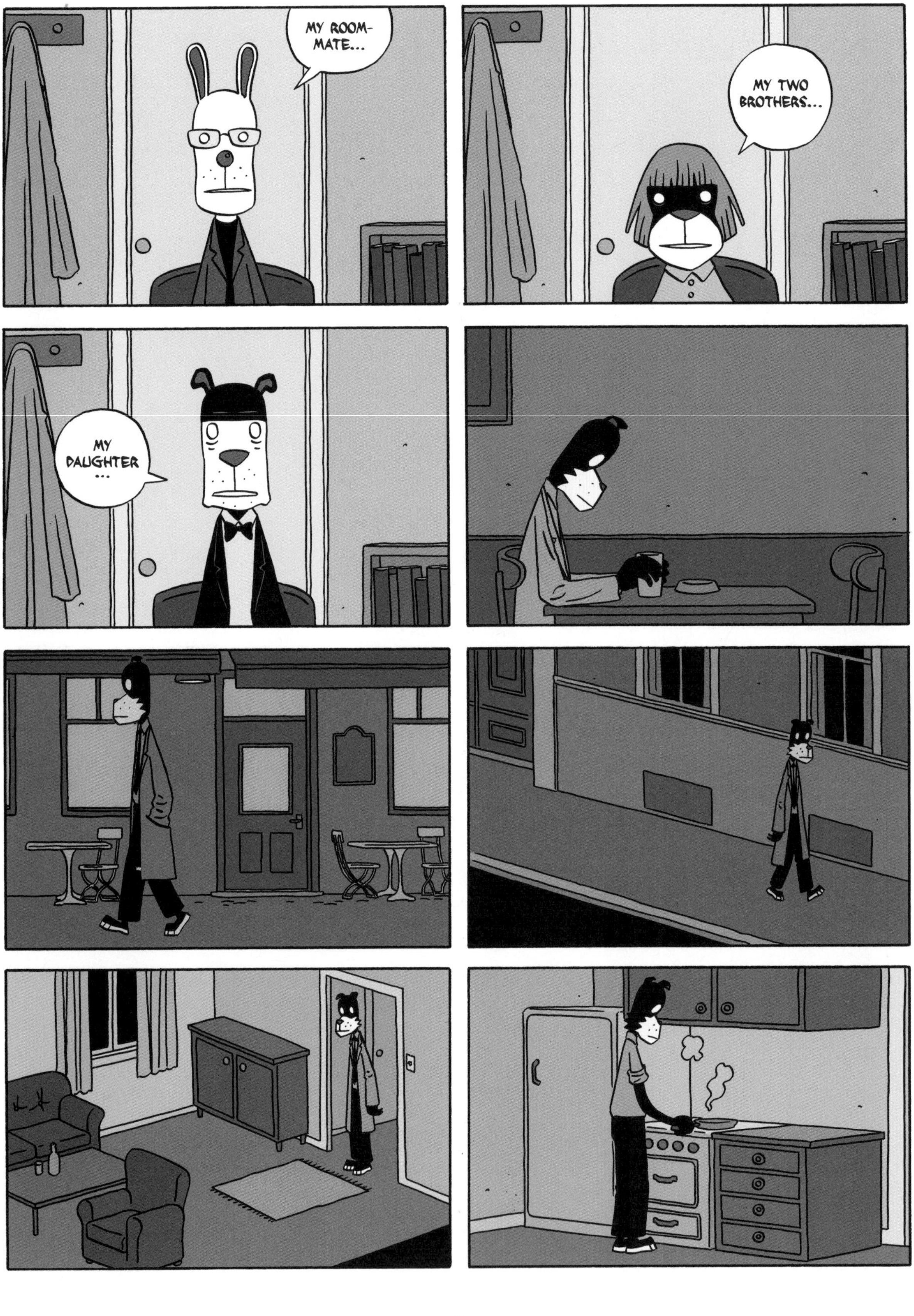
MY ROOM-
MATE...
MY TWO
BROTHERS...
MY
DAUGHTER
...

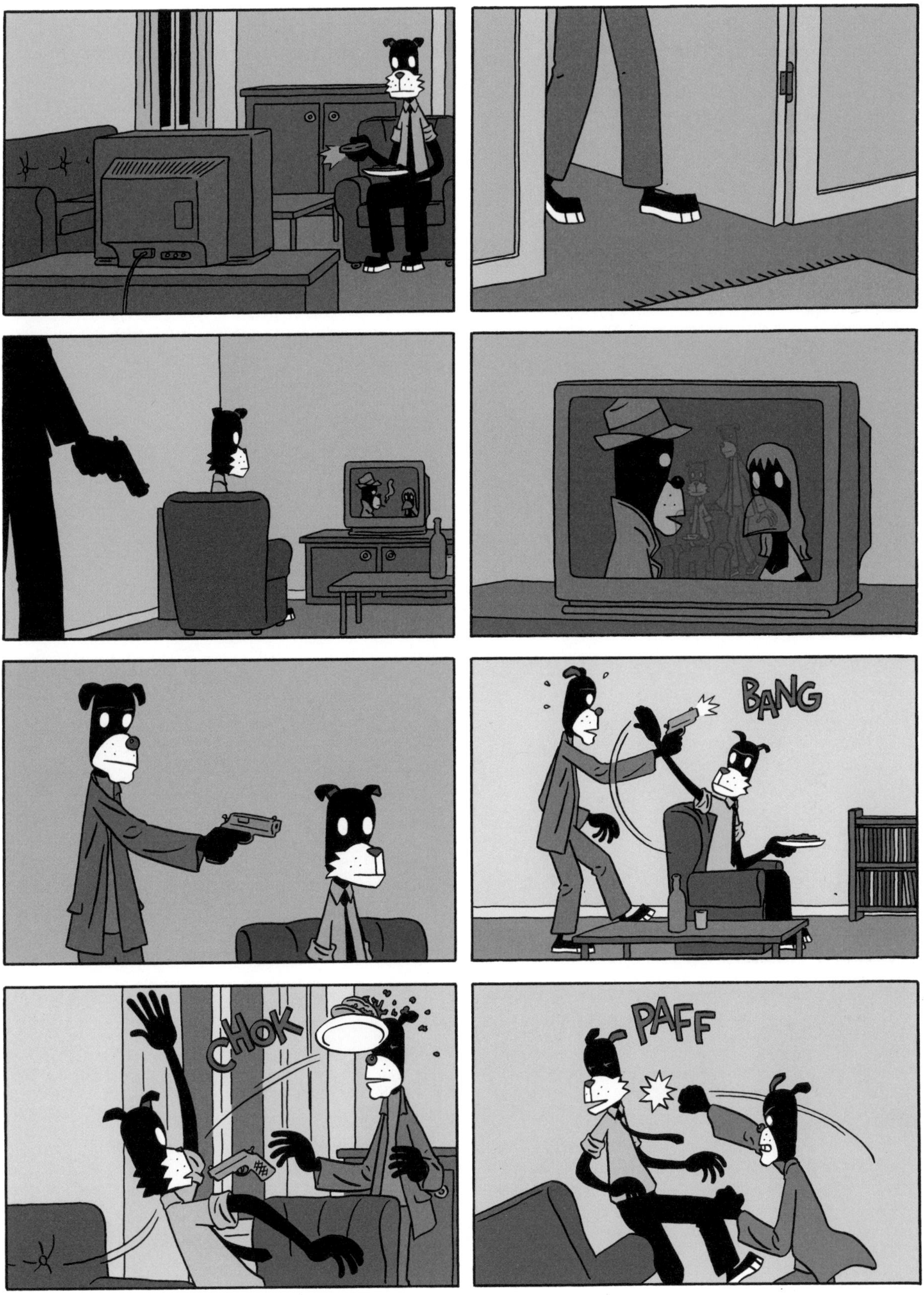
BANG
CHOK
PAFF

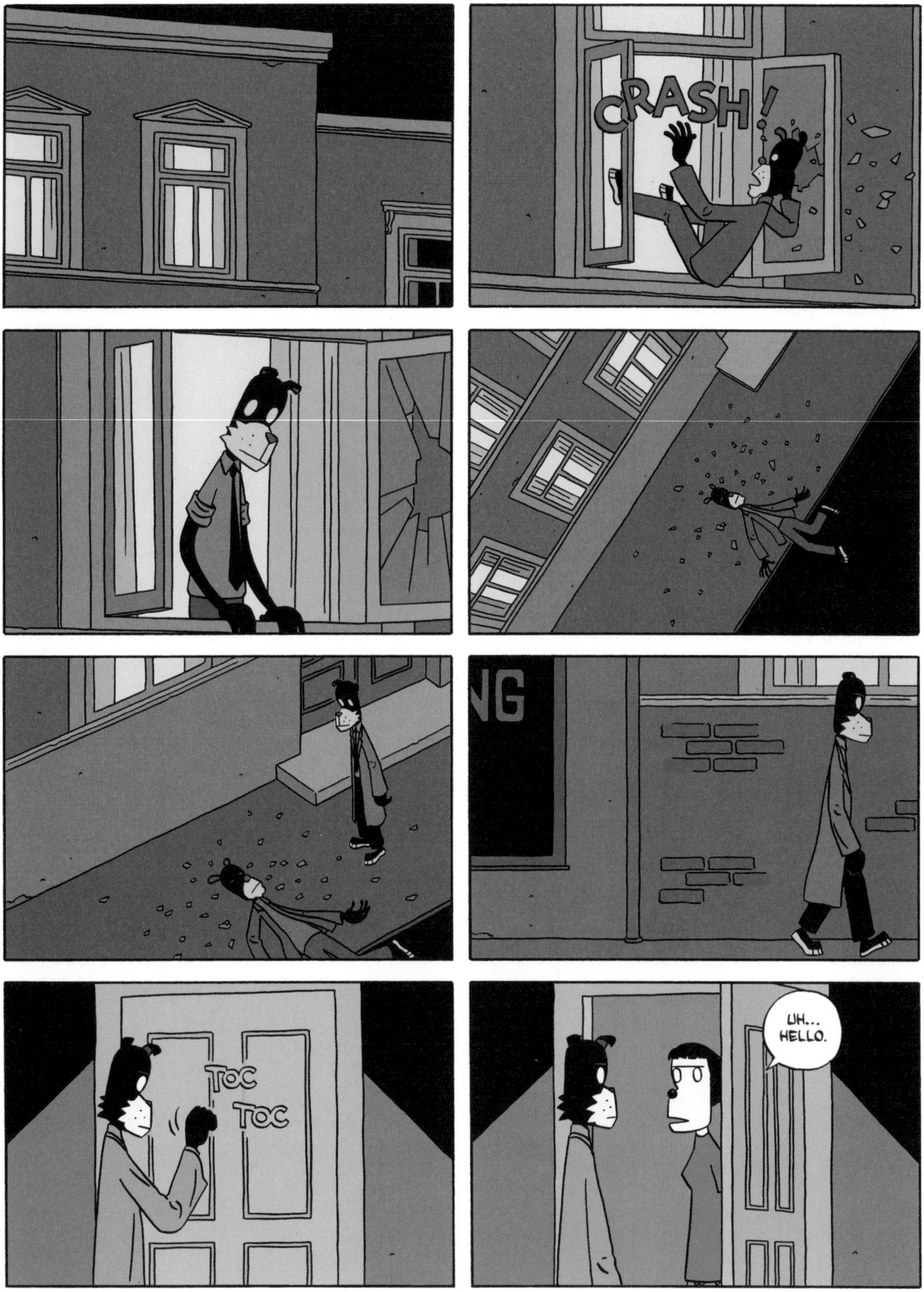
CRASH!
NG
TOC
TOC
UH... HELLO.

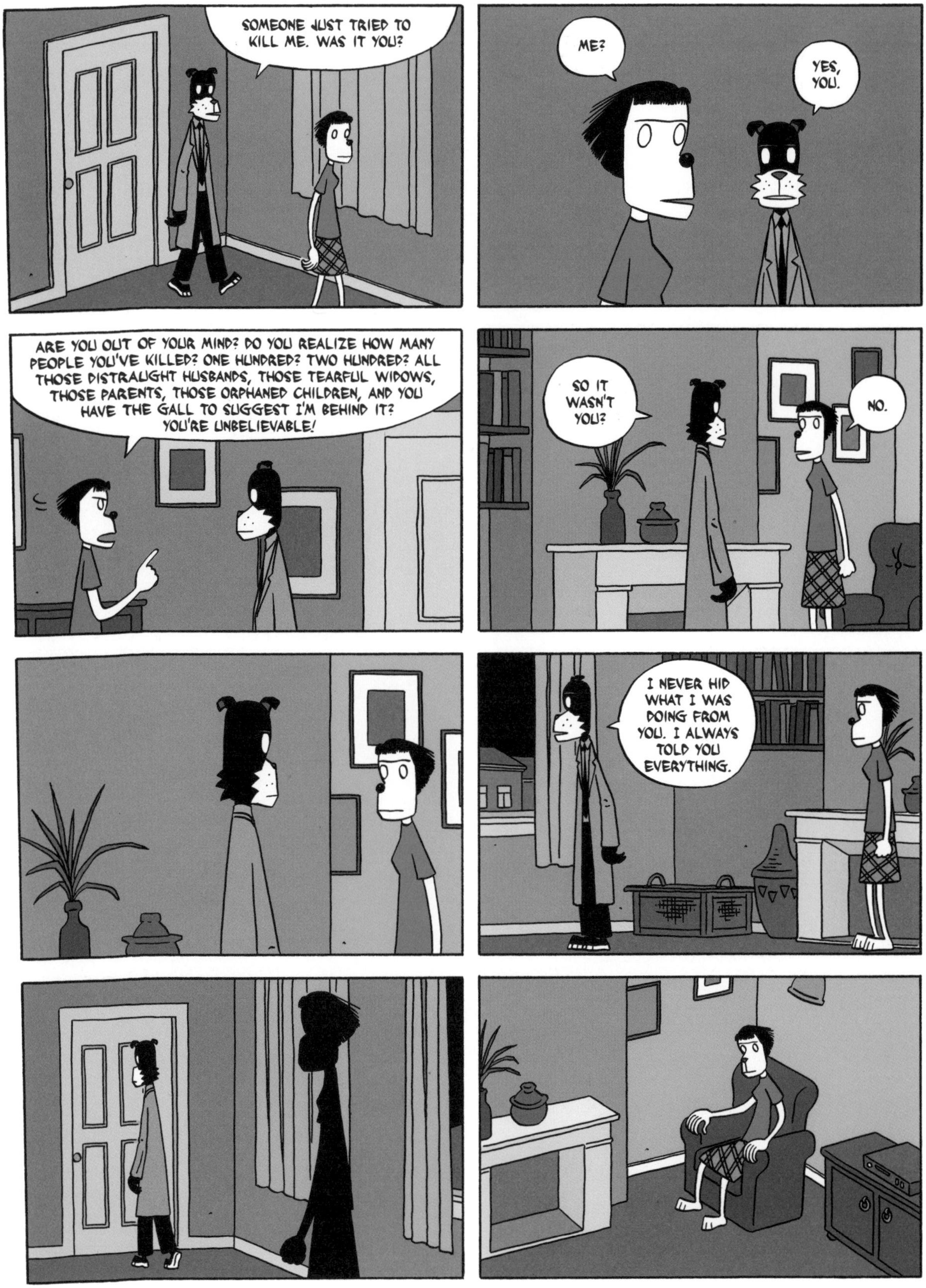
SOMEONE JUST TRIED TO KILL ME. WAS IT YOU?
ME?
YES, YOU.
ARE YOU OUT OF YOUR MIND? DO YOU REALIZE HOW MANY PEOPLE YOU'VE KILLED? ONE HUNDRED? TWO HUNDRED? ALL THOSE DISTRAUGHT HUSBANDS, THOSE TEARFUL WIDOWS, THOSE PARENTS, THOSE ORPHANED CHILDREN, AND YOU HAVE THE GALL TO SUGGEST I'M BEHIND IT? YOU'RE UNBELIEVABLE!
SO IT WASN'T YOU?
NO.
I NEVER HID WHAT I WAS DOING FROM YOU. I ALWAYS TOLD YOU EVERYTHING.

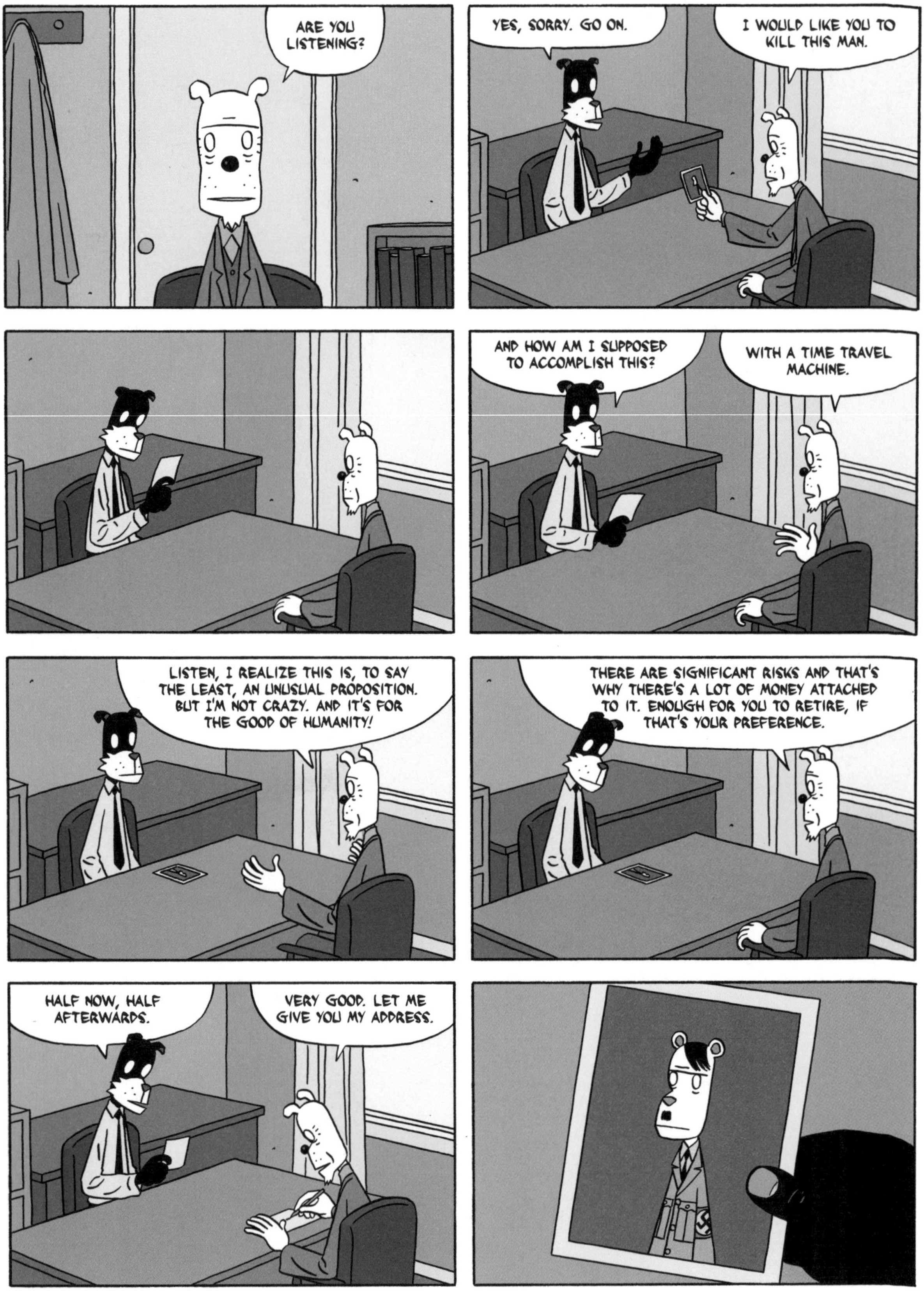
ARE YOU LISTENING?
YES, SORRY. GO ON.
I WOULD LIKE YOU TO KILL THIS MAN.
AND HOW AM I SUPPOSED TO ACCOMPLISH THIS?
WITH A TIME TRAVEL MACHINE.
LISTEN, I REALIZE THIS IS, TO SAY THE LEAST, AN UNUSUAL PROPOSITION. BUT I'M NOT CRAZY. AND IT'S FOR THE GOOD OF HUMANITY!
THERE ARE SIGNIFICANT RISKS AND THAT'S WHY THERE'S A LOT OF MONEY ATTACHED TO IT. ENOUGH FOR YOU TO RETIRE, IF THAT'S YOUR PREFERENCE.
HALF NOW, HALF AFTERWARDS.
VERY GOOD. LET ME GIVE YOU MY ADDRESS.

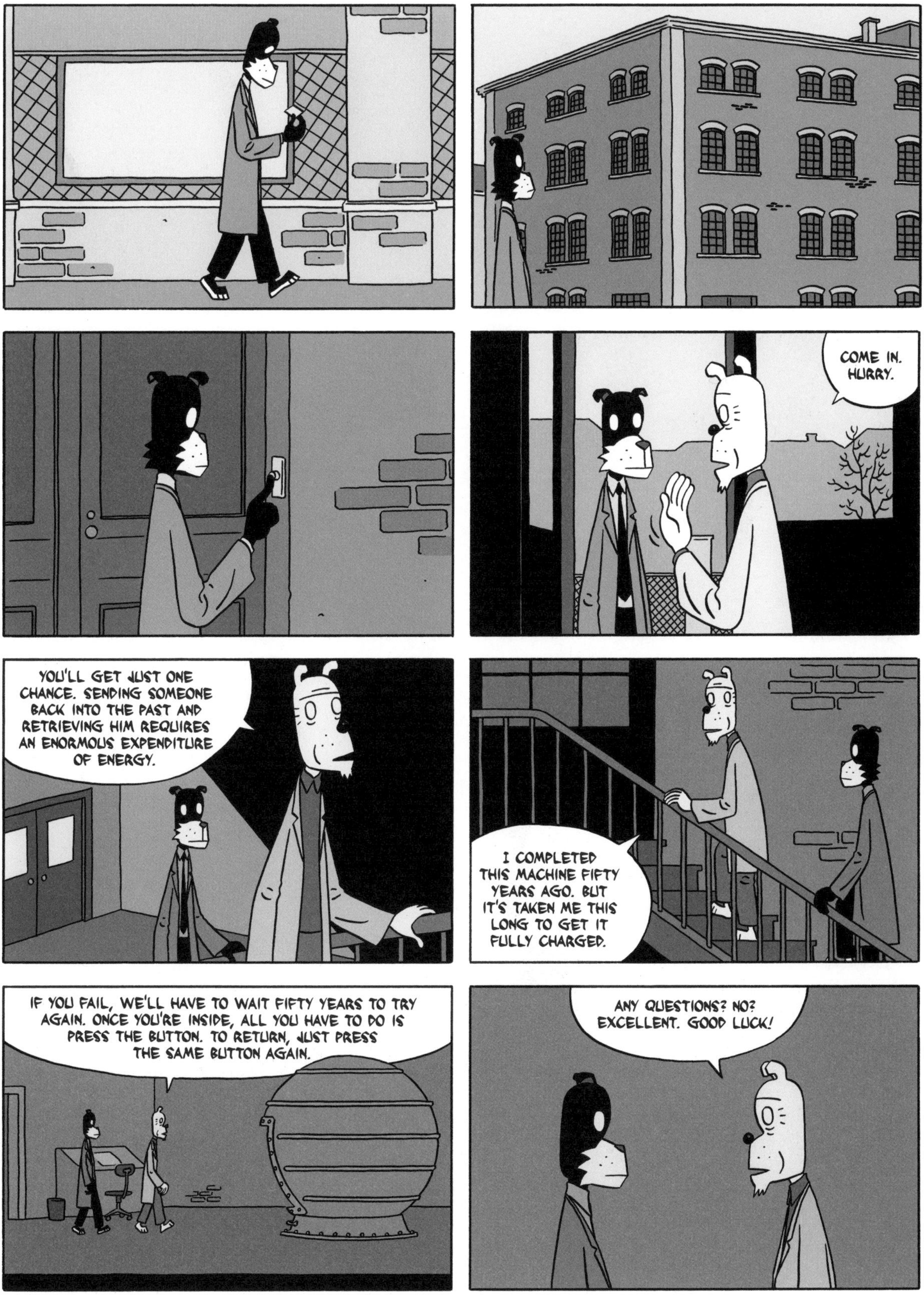
COME IN. HURRY.
YOU'LL GET JUST ONE CHANCE. SENDING SOMEONE BACK INTO THE PAST AND RETRIEVING HIM REQUIRES AN ENORMOUS EXPENDITURE OF ENERGY.
I COMPLETED THIS MACHINE FIFTY YEARS AGO. BUT IT'S TAKEN ME THIS LONG TO GET IT FULLY CHARGED.
IF YOU FAIL, WE'LL HAVE TO WAIT FIFTY YEARS TO TRY AGAIN. ONCE YOU'RE INSIDE, ALL YOU HAVE TO DO IS PRESS THE BUTTON. TO RETURN, JUST PRESS THE SAME BUTTON AGAIN.
ANY QUESTIONS? NO? EXCELLENT. GOOD LUCK!

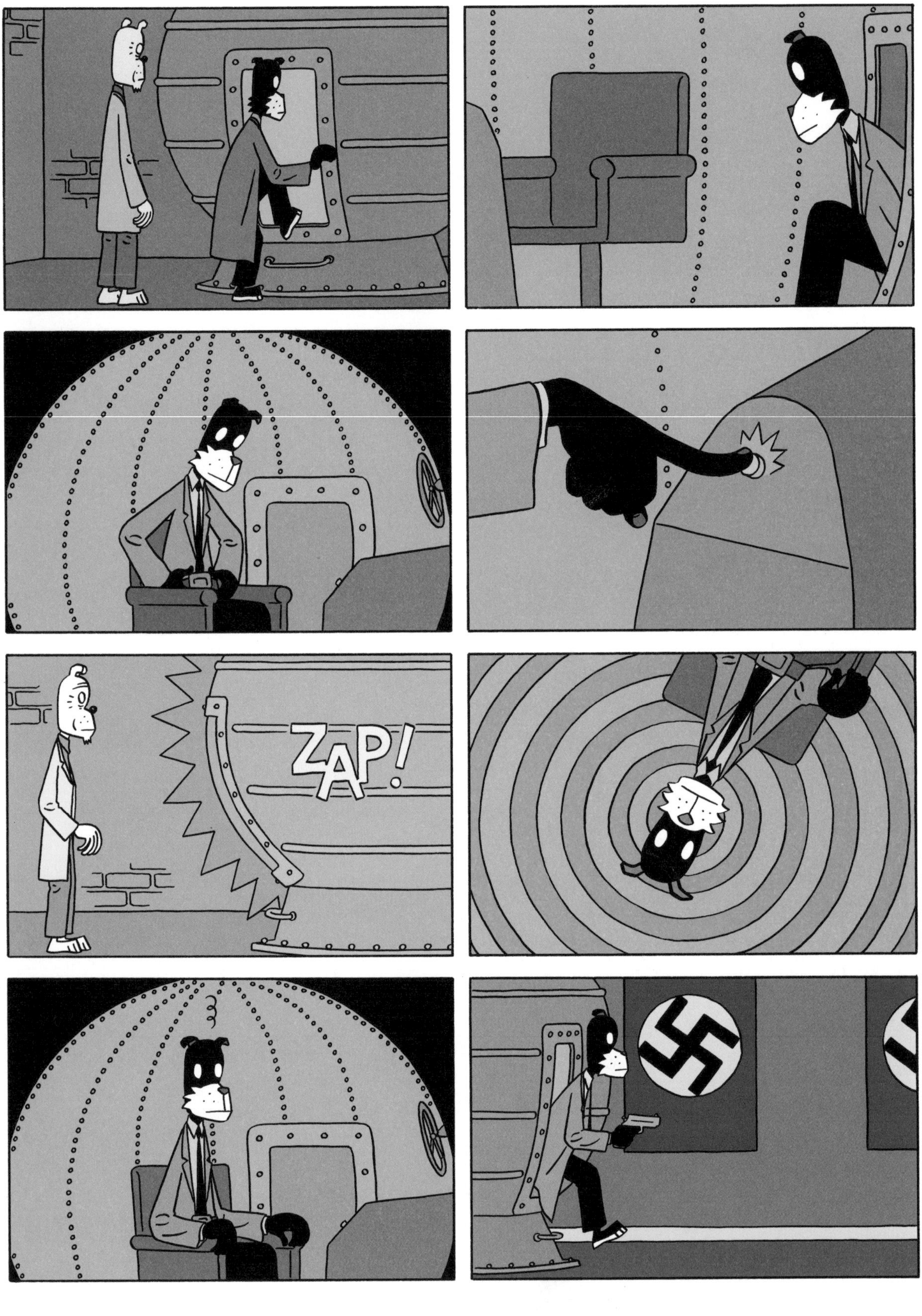
ZAP!

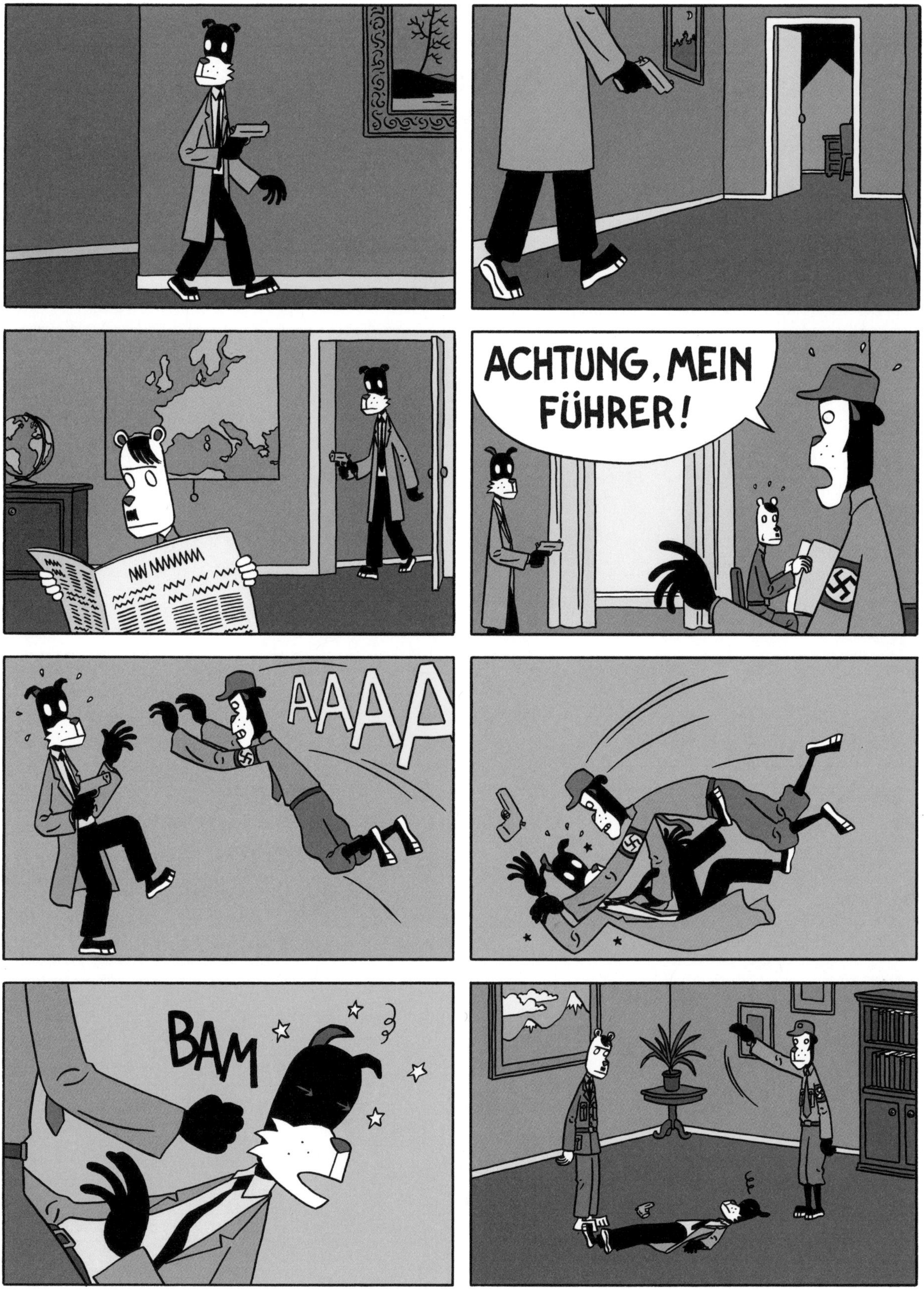
ACHTUNG, MEIN FÜHRER!
AAAA
BAM

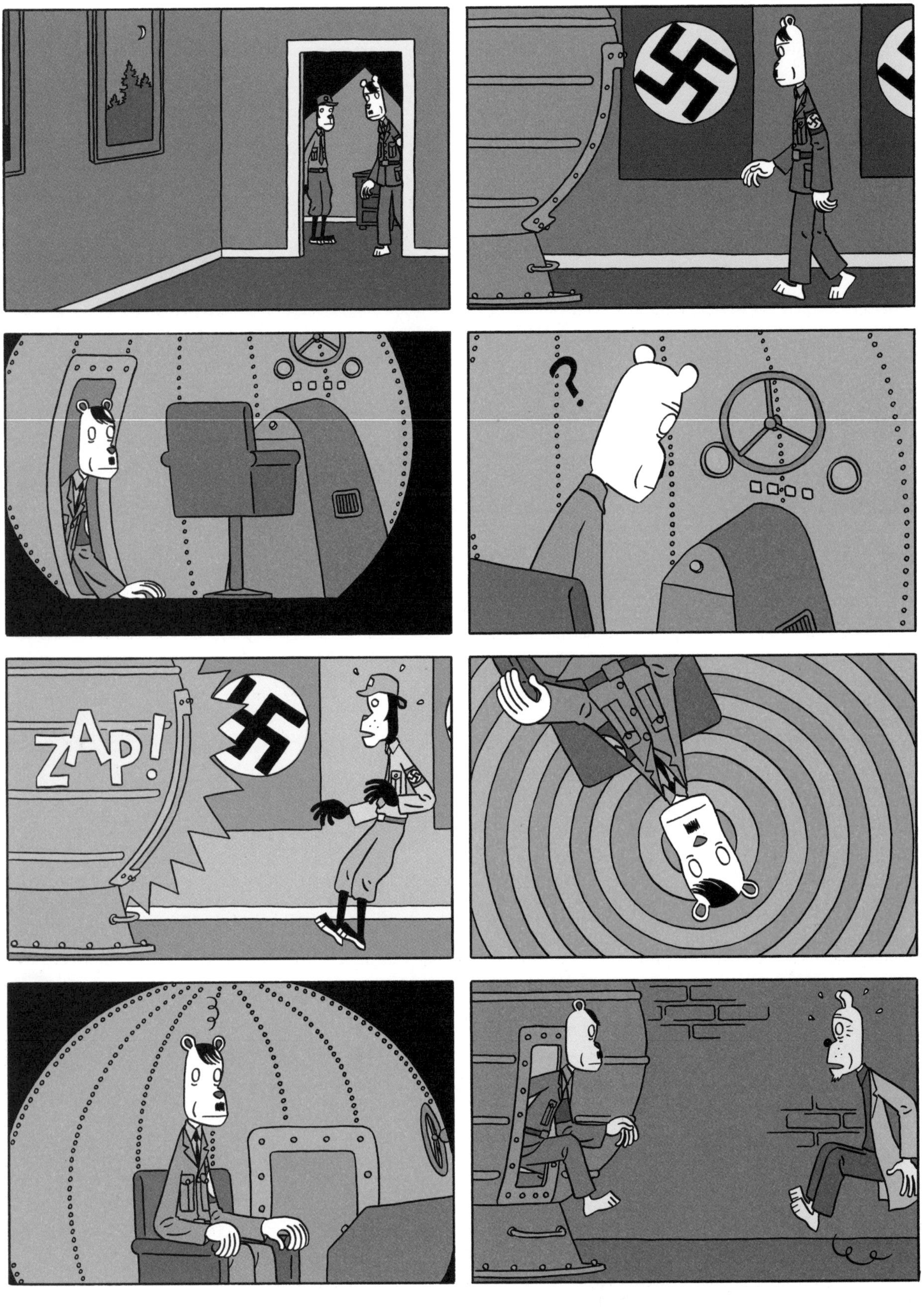
?
ZAP!

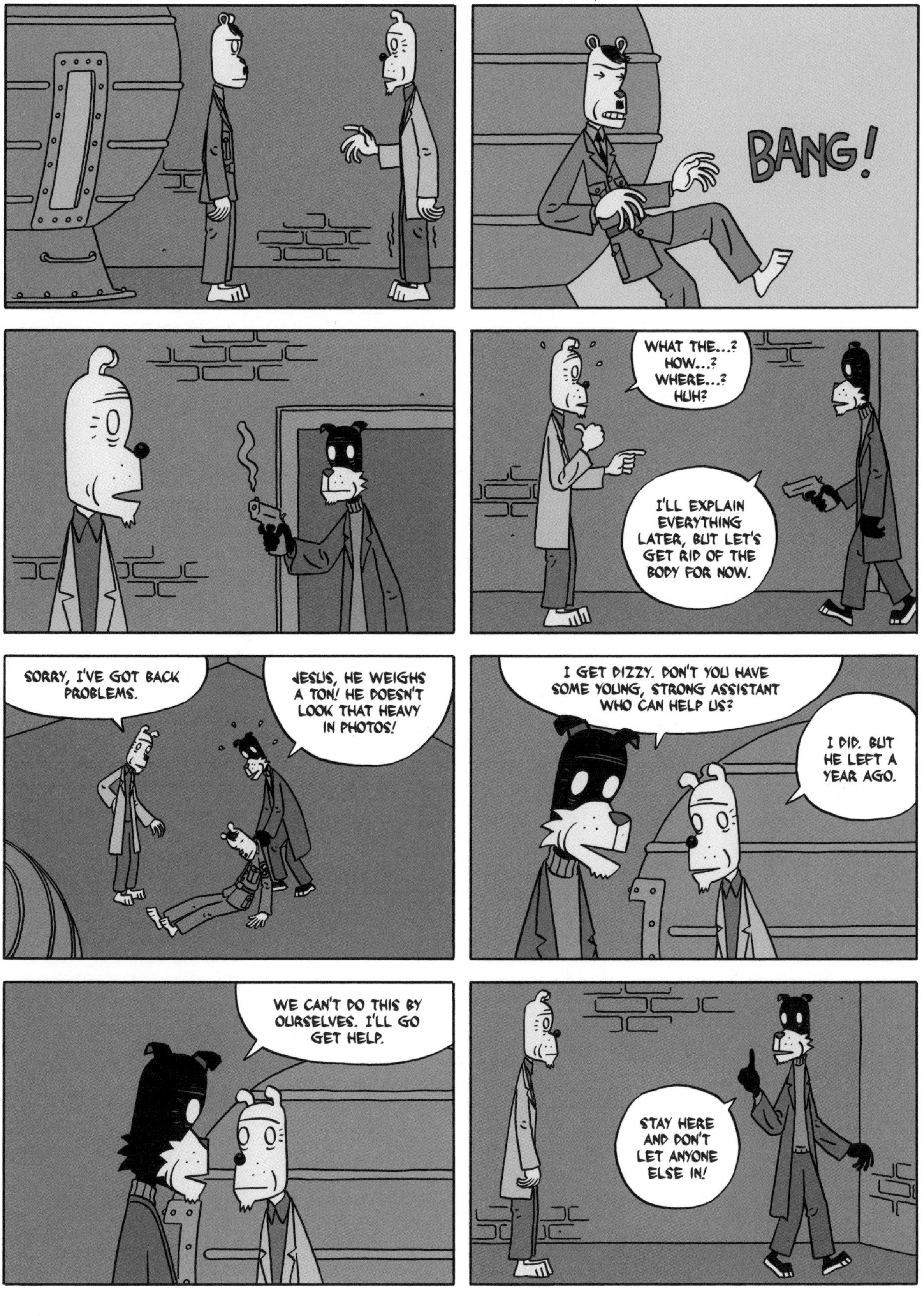
BANG!
WHAT THE...? HOW...? WHERE...? HUH?
I'LL EXPLAIN EVERYTHING LATER, BUT LET'S GET RID OF THE BODY FOR NOW.
SORRY, I'VE GOT BACK PROBLEMS.
JESUS, HE WEIGHS A TON! HE DOESN'T LOOK THAT HEAVY IN PHOTOS!
I GET DIZZY. DON'T YOU HAVE SOME YOUNG, STRONG ASSISTANT WHO CAN HELP US?
I DID. BUT HE LEFT A YEAR AGO.
WE CAN'T DO THIS BY OURSELVES. I'LL GO GET HELP.
STAY HERE AND DON'T LET ANYONE ELSE IN!

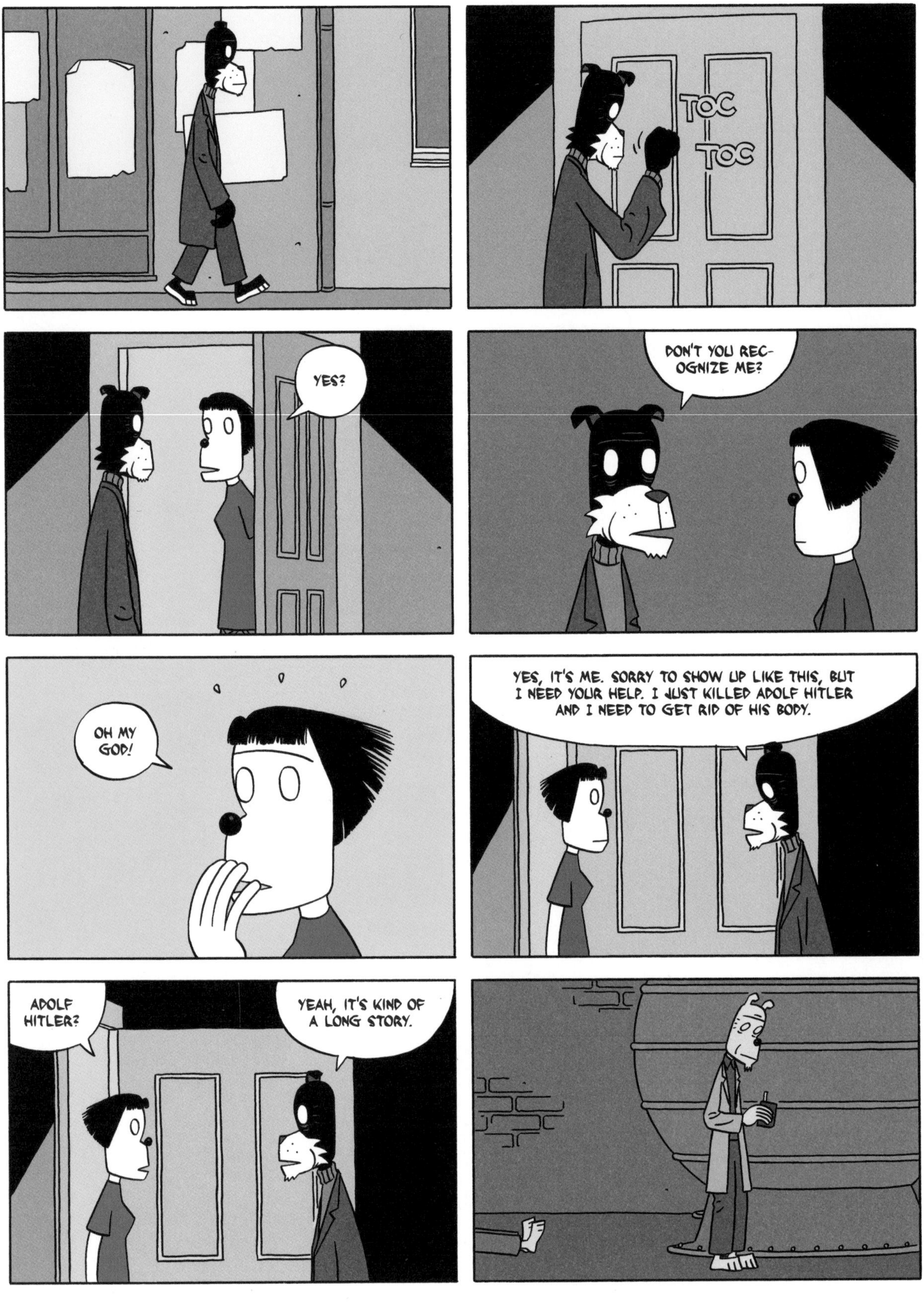
TOC
TOC
YES?
DON'T YOU REC-
OGNIZE ME?
OH MY
GOD!
YES, IT'S ME. SORRY TO SHOW UP LIKE THIS, BUT
I NEED YOUR HELP. I JUST KILLED ADOLF HITLER
AND I NEED TO GET RID OF HIS BODY.
ADOLF
HITLER?
YEAH, IT'S KIND OF
A LONG STORY.

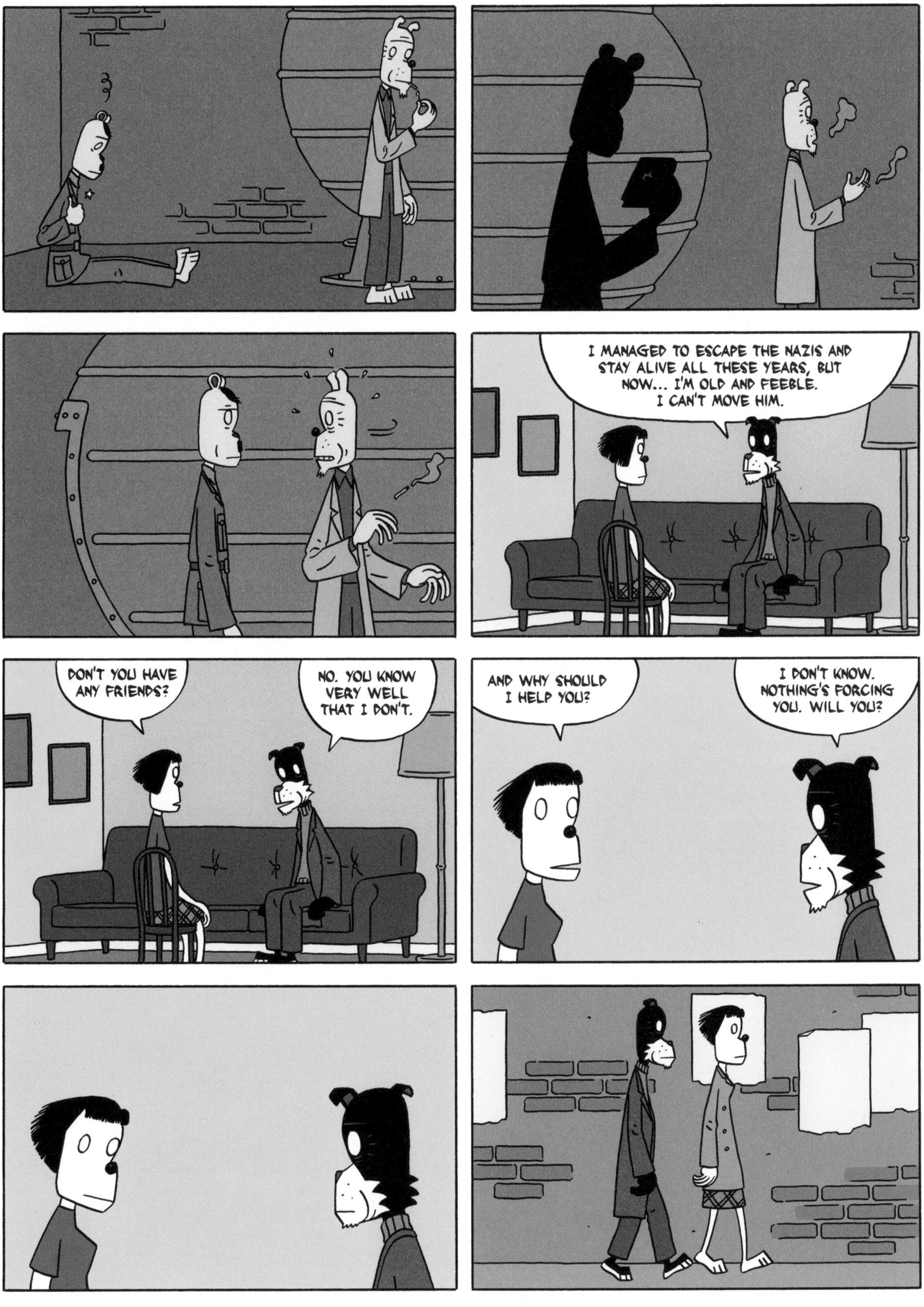
I MANAGED TO ESCAPE THE NAZIS AND STAY ALIVE ALL THESE YEARS, BUT NOW... I'M OLD AND FEEBLE. I CAN'T MOVE HIM.
DON'T YOU HAVE ANY FRIENDS?
NO. YOU KNOW VERY WELL THAT I DON'T.
AND WHY SHOULD I HELP YOU?
I DON'T KNOW. NOTHING'S FORCING YOU. WILL YOU?

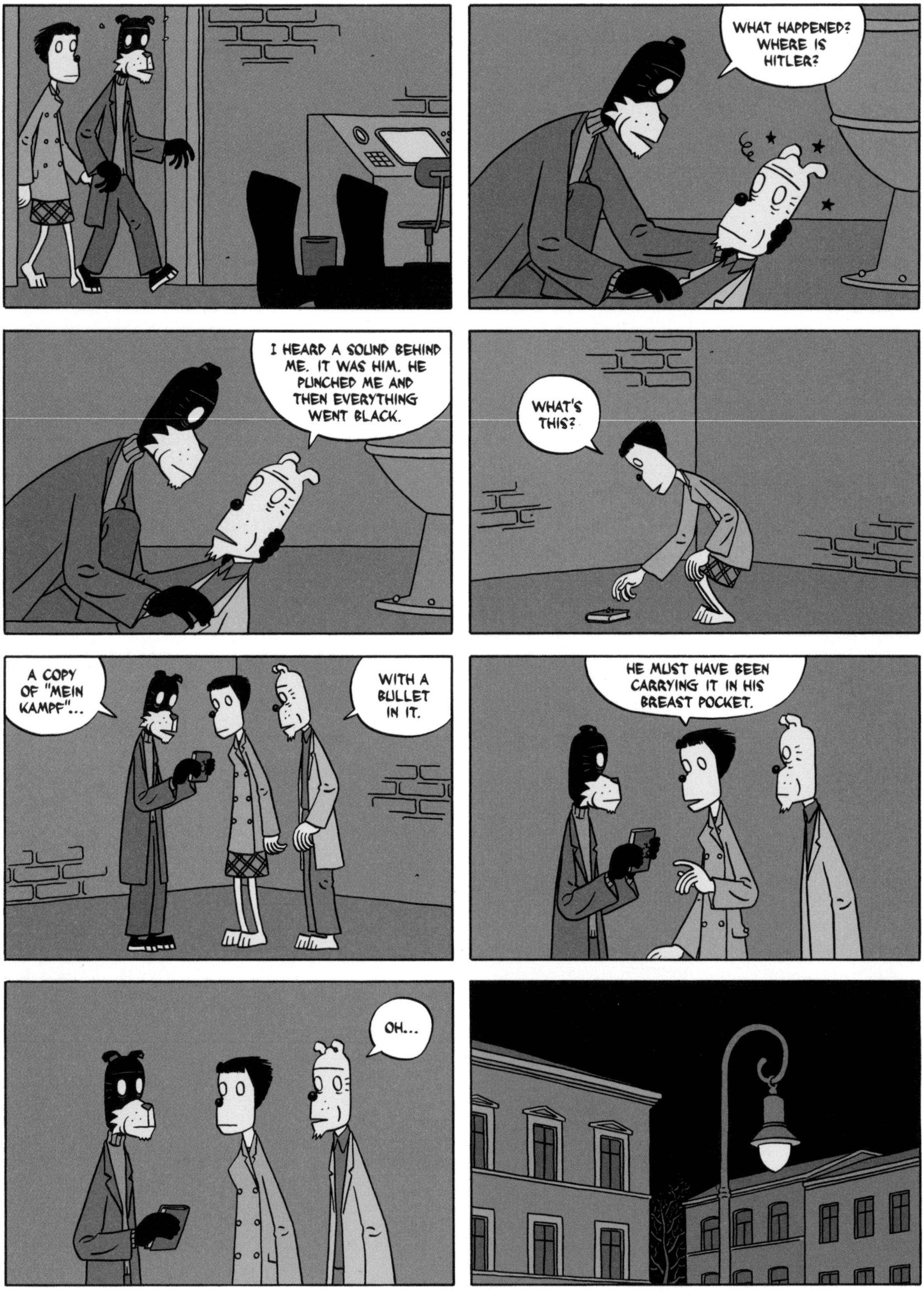
WHAT HAPPENED? WHERE IS HITLER?
I HEARD A SOUND BEHIND ME. IT WAS HIM. HE PUNCHED ME AND THEN EVERYTHING WENT BLACK.
WHAT'S THIS?
A COPY OF "MEIN KAMPF"...
WITH A BULLET IN IT.
HE MUST HAVE BEEN CARRYING IT IN HIS BREAST POCKET.
OH...

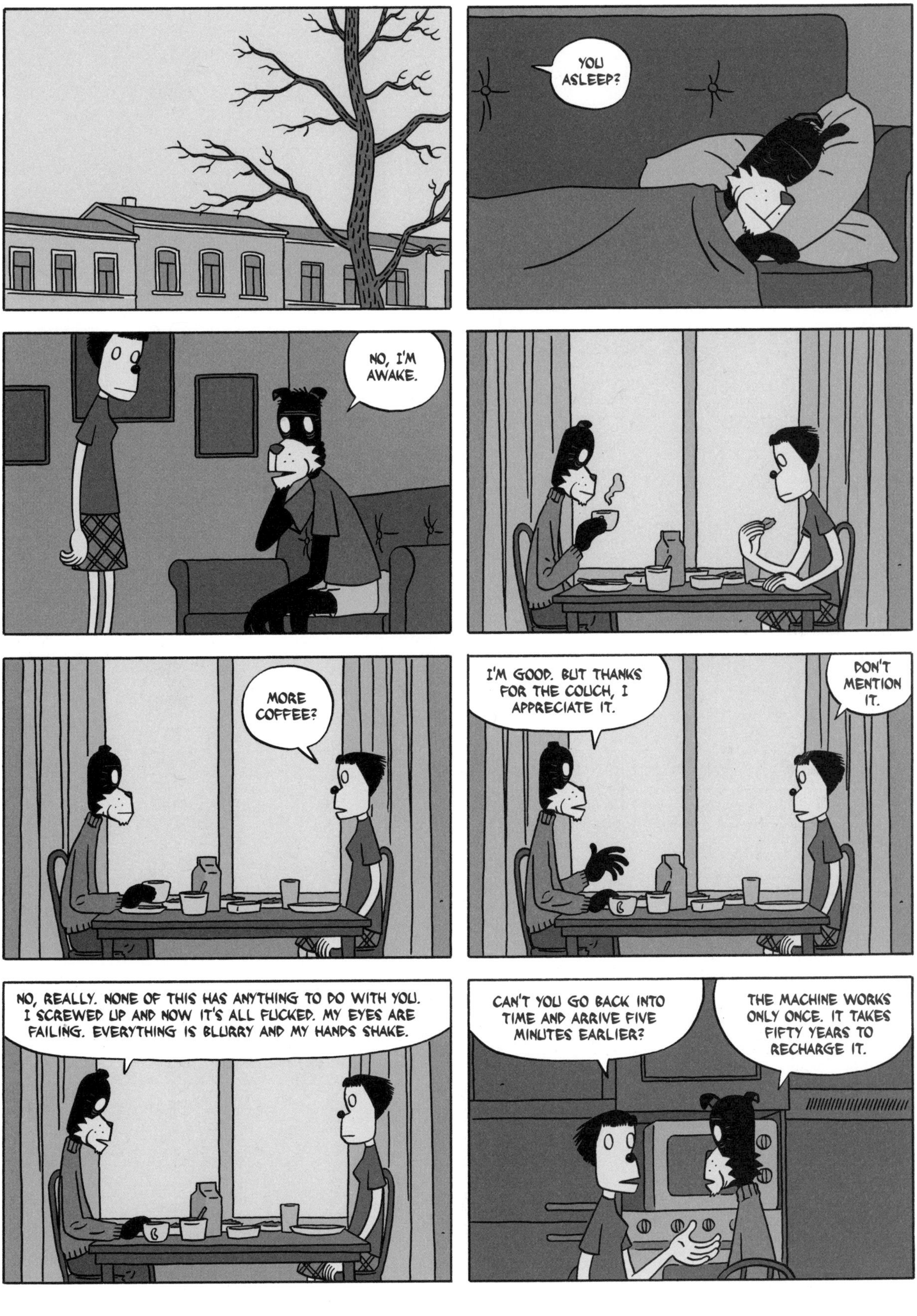
YOU ASLEEP?
NO, I'M AWAKE.
MORE COFFEE?
I'M GOOD. BUT THANKS FOR THE COUCH, I APPRECIATE IT.
DON'T MENTION IT.
NO, REALLY. NONE OF THIS HAS ANYTHING TO DO WITH YOU. I SCREWED UP AND NOW IT'S ALL FUCKED. MY EYES ARE FAILING. EVERYTHING IS BLURRY AND MY HANDS SHAKE.
CAN'T YOU GO BACK INTO TIME AND ARRIVE FIVE MINUTES EARLIER?
THE MACHINE WORKS ONLY ONCE. IT TAKES FIFTY YEARS TO RECHARGE IT.

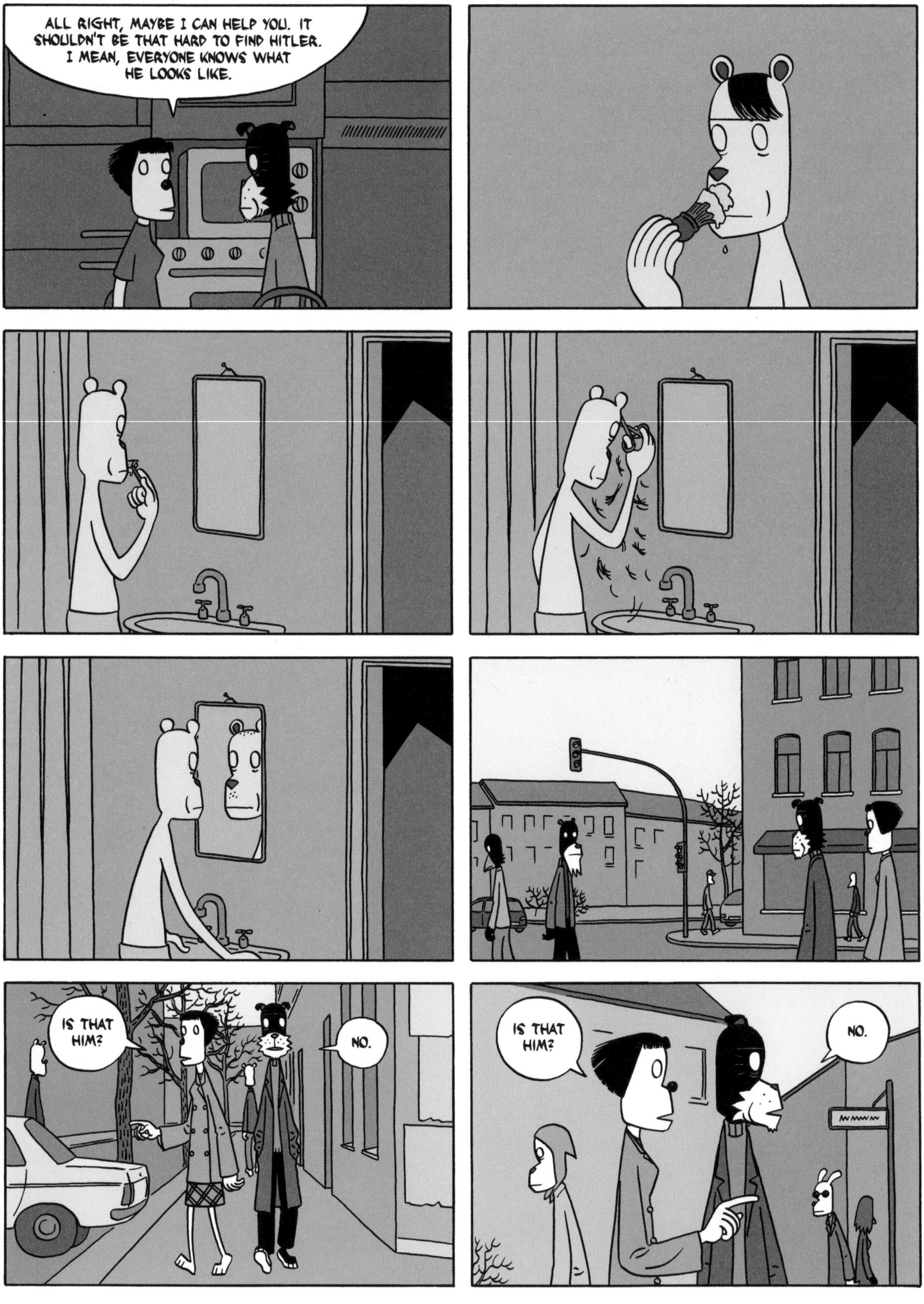
ALL RIGHT, MAYBE I CAN HELP YOU. IT SHOULDN'T BE THAT HARD TO FIND HITLER. I MEAN, EVERYONE KNOWS WHAT HE LOOKS LIKE.
IS THAT HIM?
NO.
IS THAT HIM?
NO.

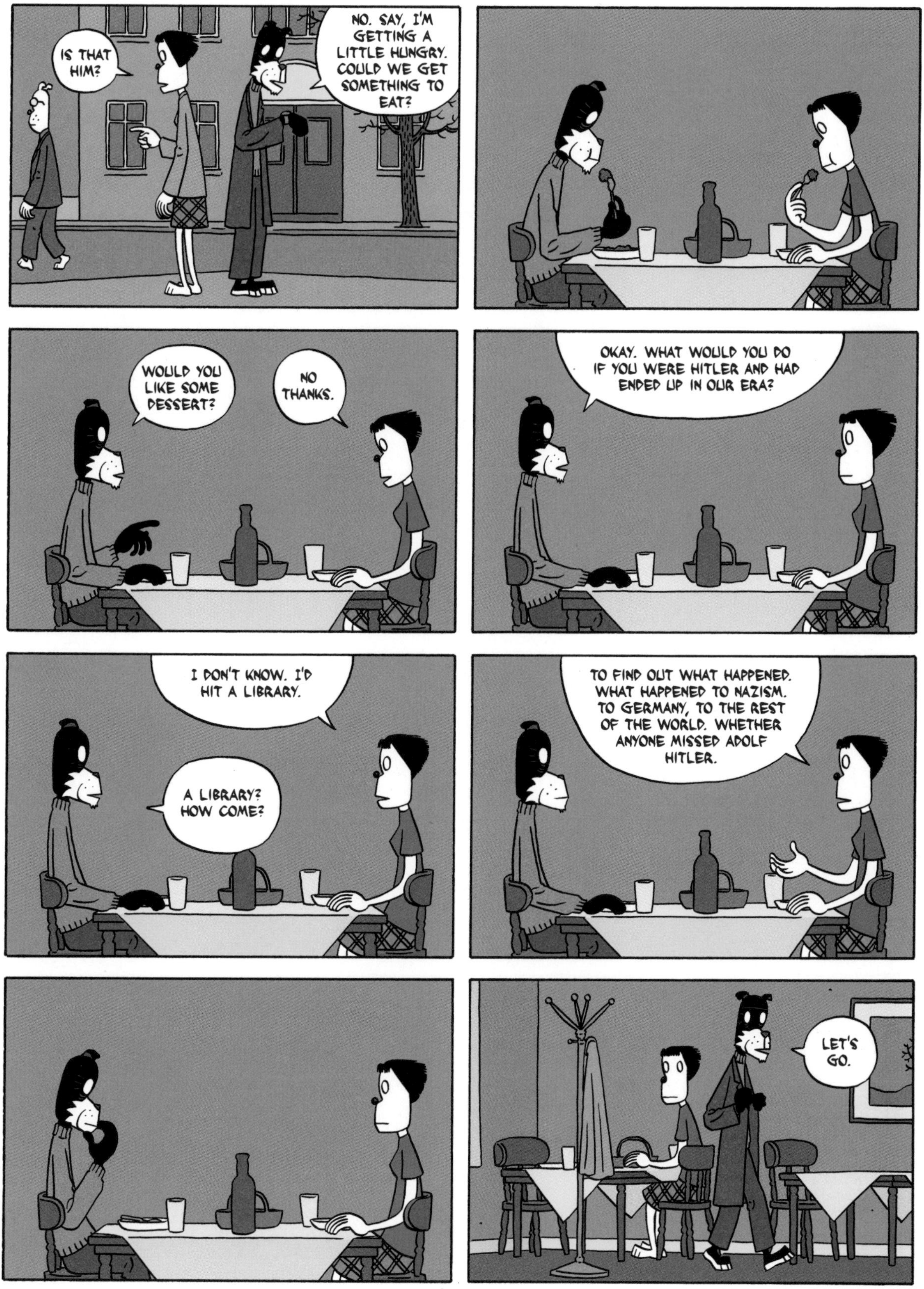
IS THAT HIM?
NO. SAY, I'M GETTING A LITTLE HUNGRY. COULD WE GET SOMETHING TO EAT?
WOULD YOU LIKE SOME DESSERT?
NO THANKS.
OKAY. WHAT WOULD YOU DO IF YOU WERE HITLER AND HAD ENDED UP IN OUR ERA?
I DON'T KNOW. I'D HIT A LIBRARY.
A LIBRARY? HOW COME?
TO FIND OUT WHAT HAPPENED. WHAT HAPPENED TO NAZISM. TO GERMANY, TO THE REST OF THE WORLD. WHETHER ANYONE MISSED ADOLF HITLER.
LET'S GO.

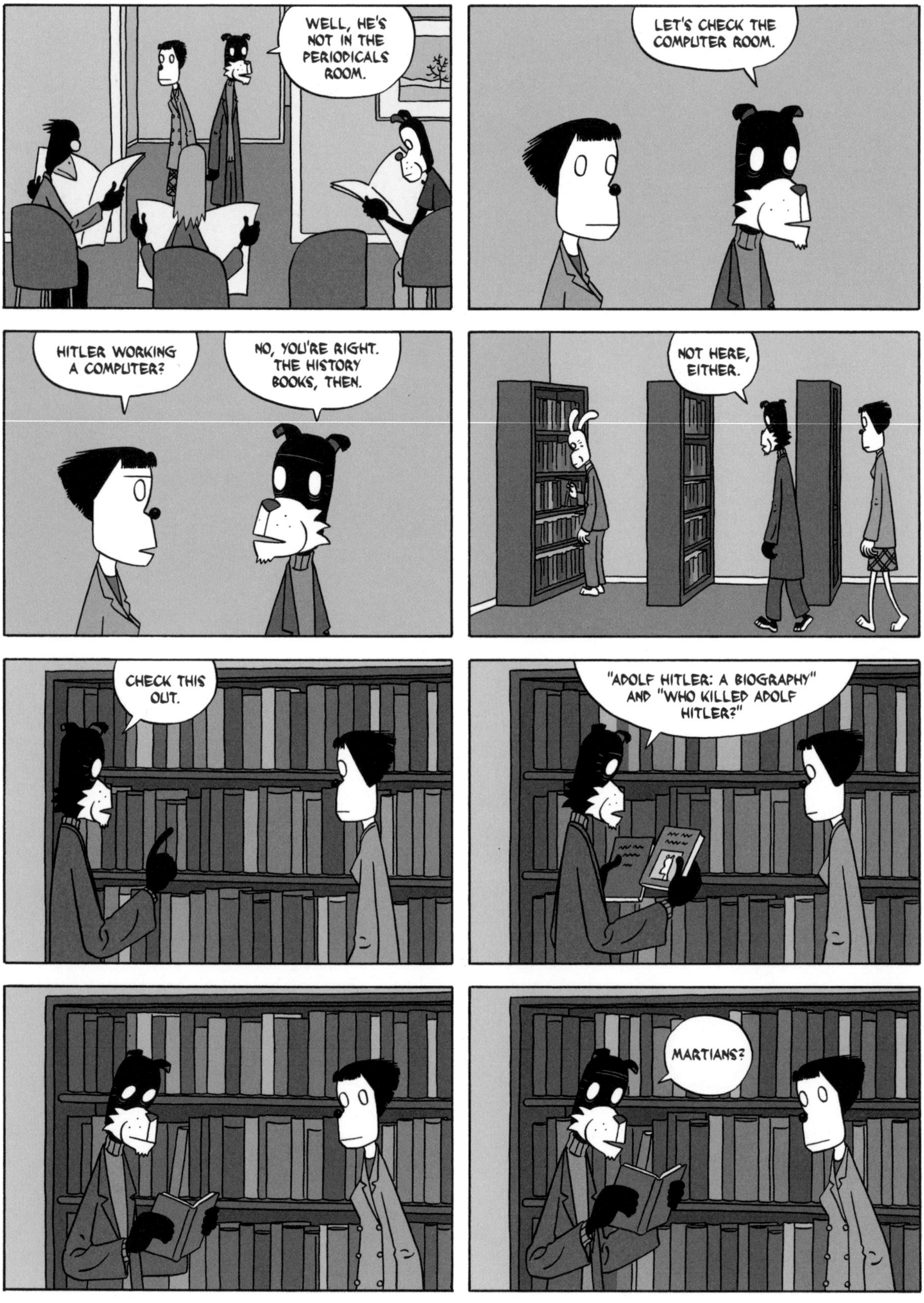
WELL, HE'S NOT IN THE PERIODICALS ROOM.
LET'S CHECK THE COMPUTER ROOM.
HITLER WORKING A COMPUTER?
NO, YOU'RE RIGHT. THE HISTORY BOOKS, THEN.
NOT HERE, EITHER.
CHECK THIS OUT.
"ADOLF HITLER: A BIOGRAPHY" AND "WHO KILLED ADOLF HITLER?"
MARTIANS?

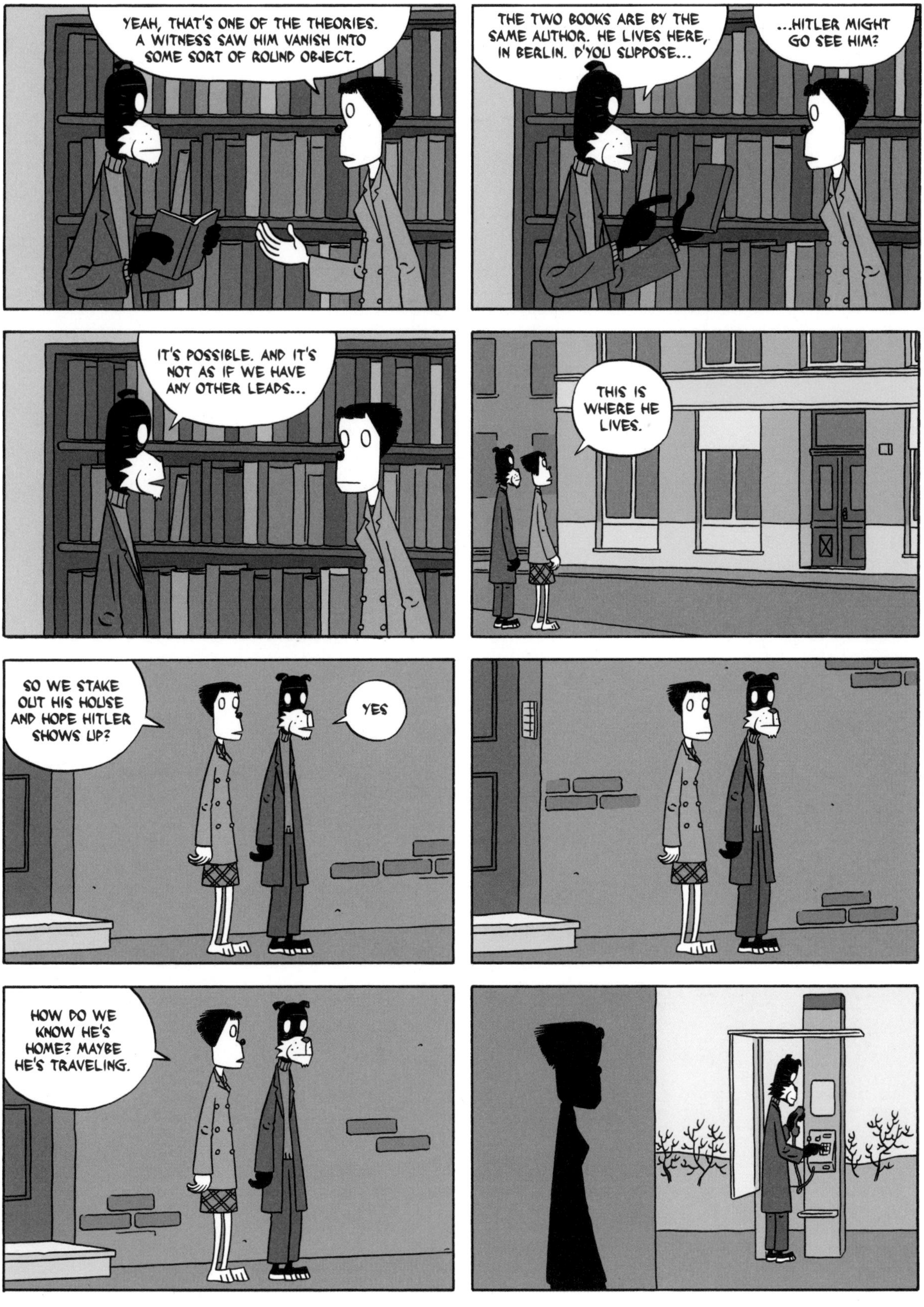
YEAH, THAT'S ONE OF THE THEORIES. A WITNESS SAW HIM VANISH INTO SOME SORT OF ROUND OBJECT.
THE TWO BOOKS ARE BY THE SAME AUTHOR. HE LIVES HERE, IN BERLIN. D'YOU SUPPOSE...
...HITLER MIGHT GO SEE HIM?
IT'S POSSIBLE. AND IT'S NOT AS IF WE HAVE ANY OTHER LEADS...
THIS IS WHERE HE LIVES.
SO WE STAKE OUT HIS HOUSE AND HOPE HITLER SHOWS UP?
YES
HOW DO WE KNOW HE'S HOME? MAYBE HE'S TRAVELING.

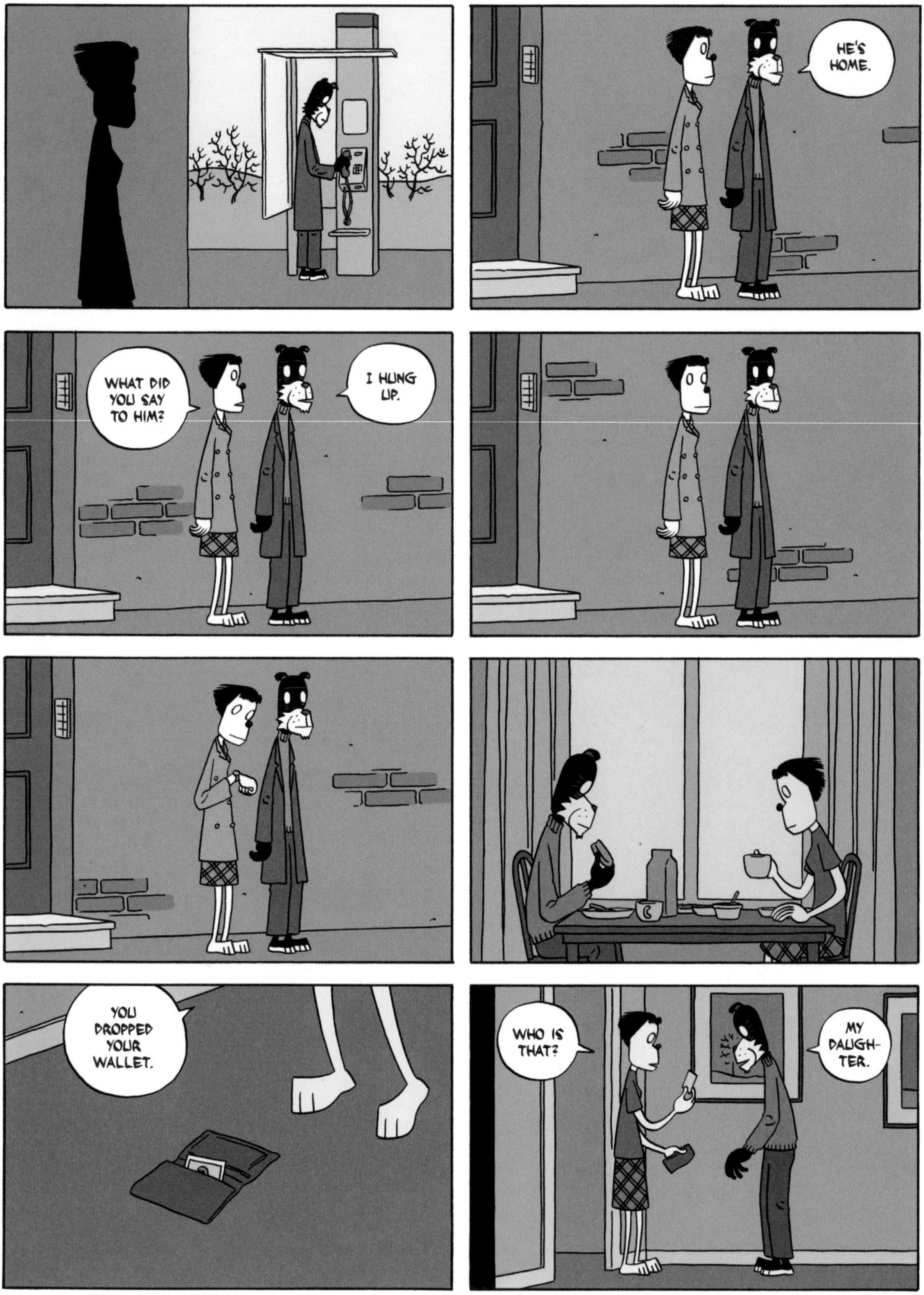
HE'S HOME.
WHAT DID YOU SAY TO HIM?
I HUNG UP.
YOU DROPPED YOUR WALLET.
WHO IS THAT?
MY DAUGHTER.

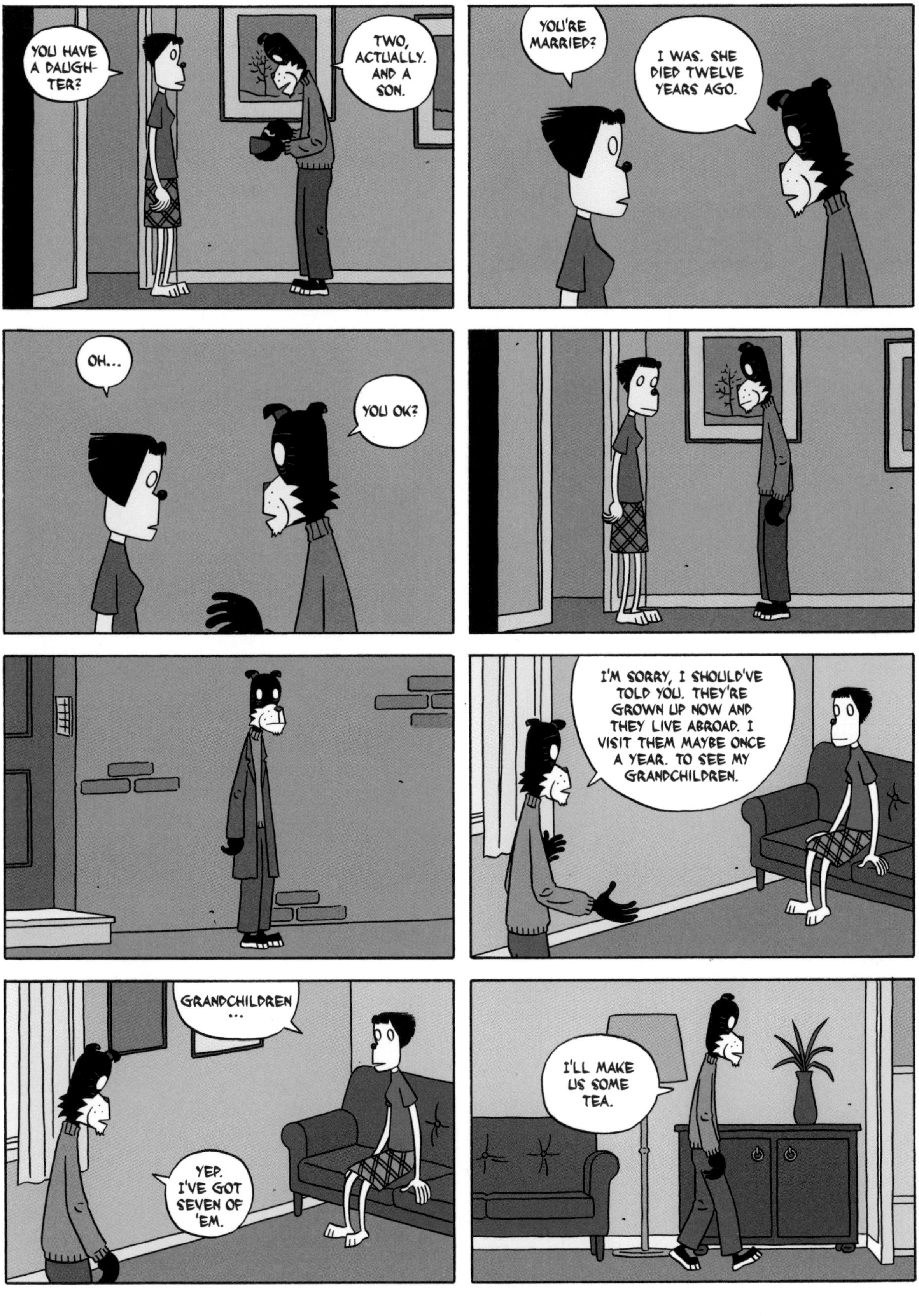
YOU HAVE A DAUGHTER?
TWO, ACTUALLY. AND A SON.
YOU'RE MARRIED?
I WAS. SHE DIED TWELVE YEARS AGO.
OH...
YOU OK?
I'M SORRY, I SHOULD'VE TOLD YOU. THEY'RE GROWN UP NOW AND THEY LIVE ABROAD. I VISIT THEM MAYBE ONCE A YEAR. TO SEE MY GRANDCHILDREN.
GRANDCHILDREN...
YEP. I'VE GOT SEVEN OF 'EM.
I'LL MAKE US SOME TEA.

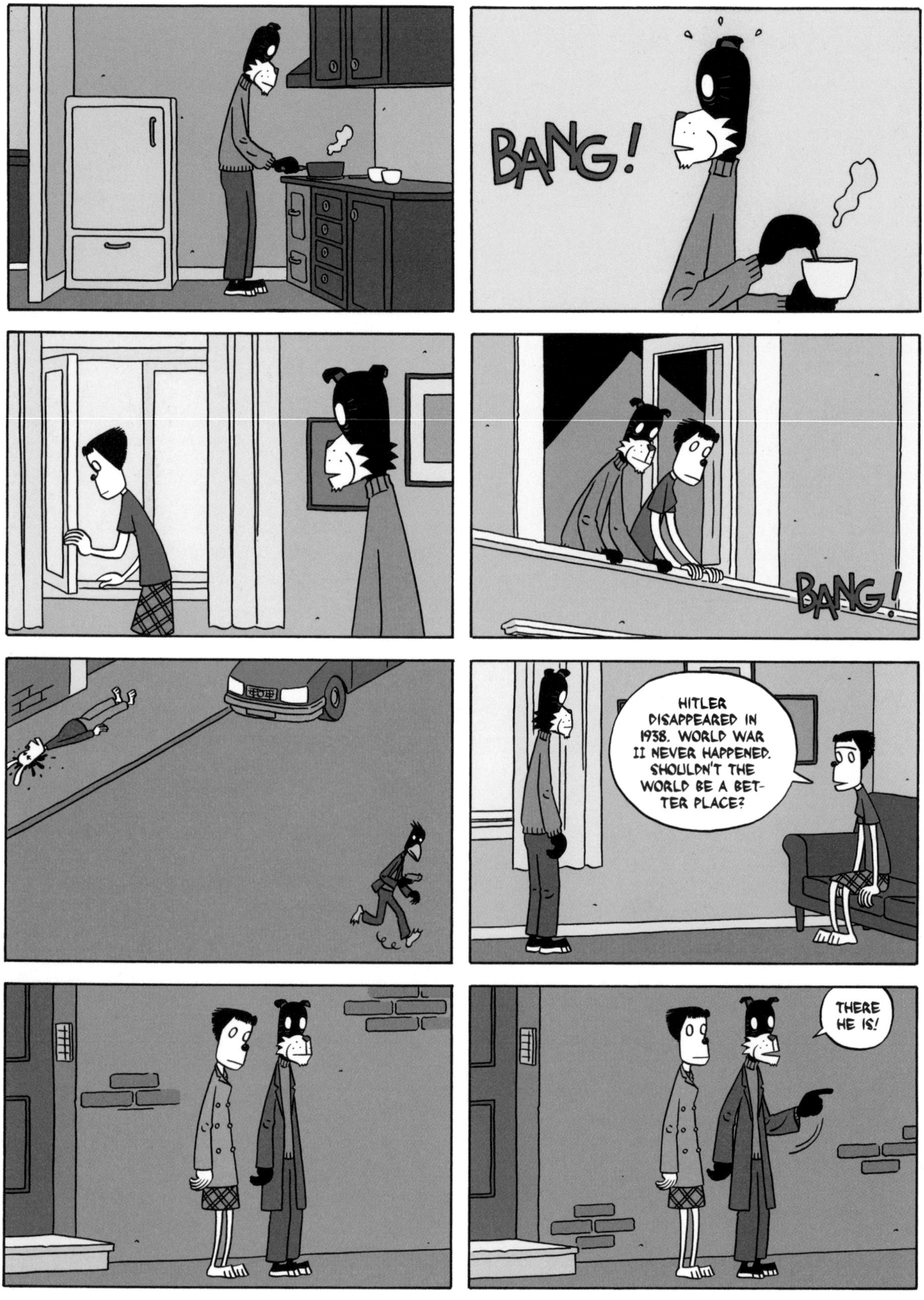
BANG!
BANG!
HITLER DISAPPEARED IN 1938. WORLD WAR II NEVER HAPPENED. SHOULDN'T THE WORLD BE A BETTER PLACE?
THERE HE IS!

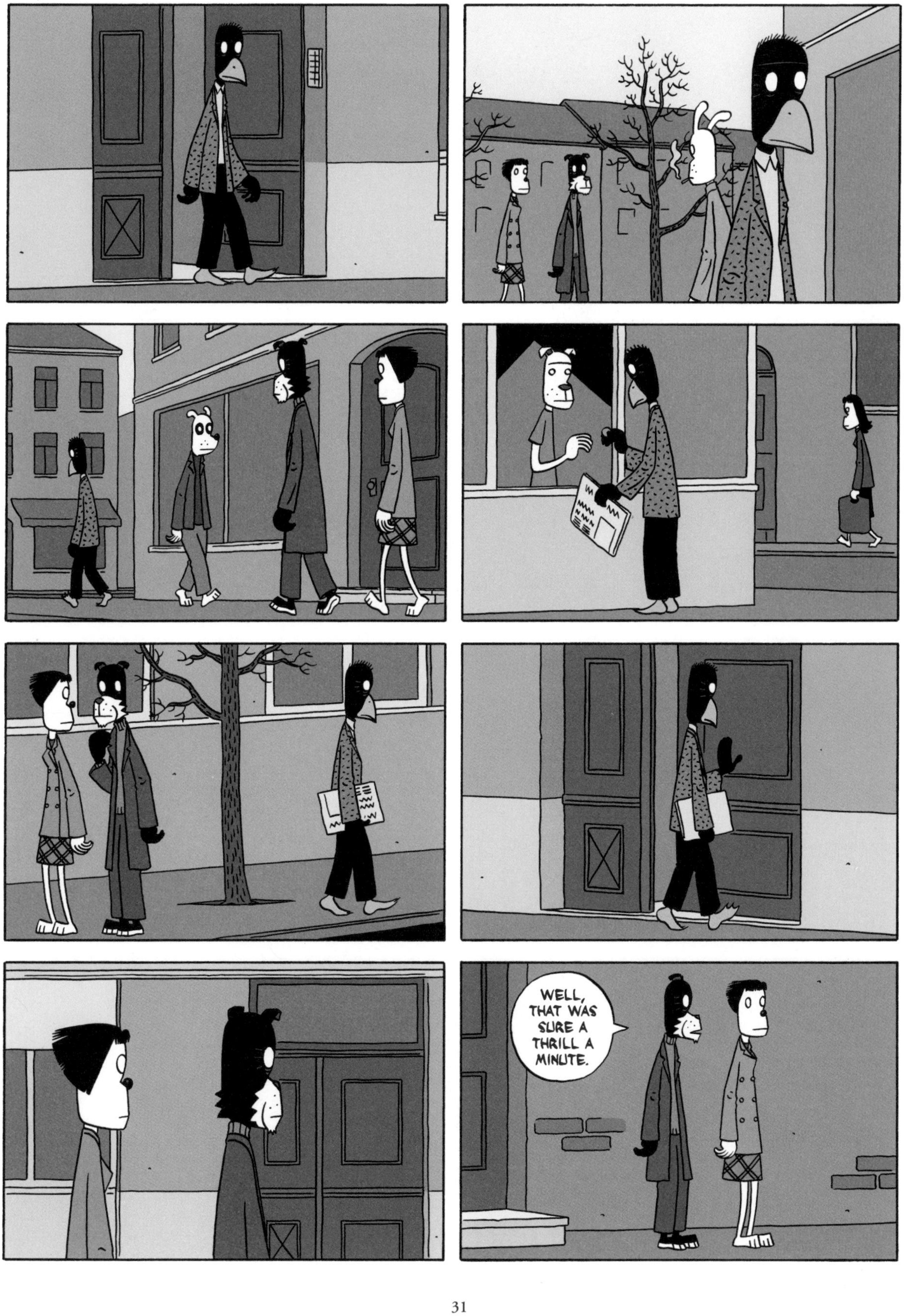
WELL, THAT WAS SURE A THRILL A MINUTE.

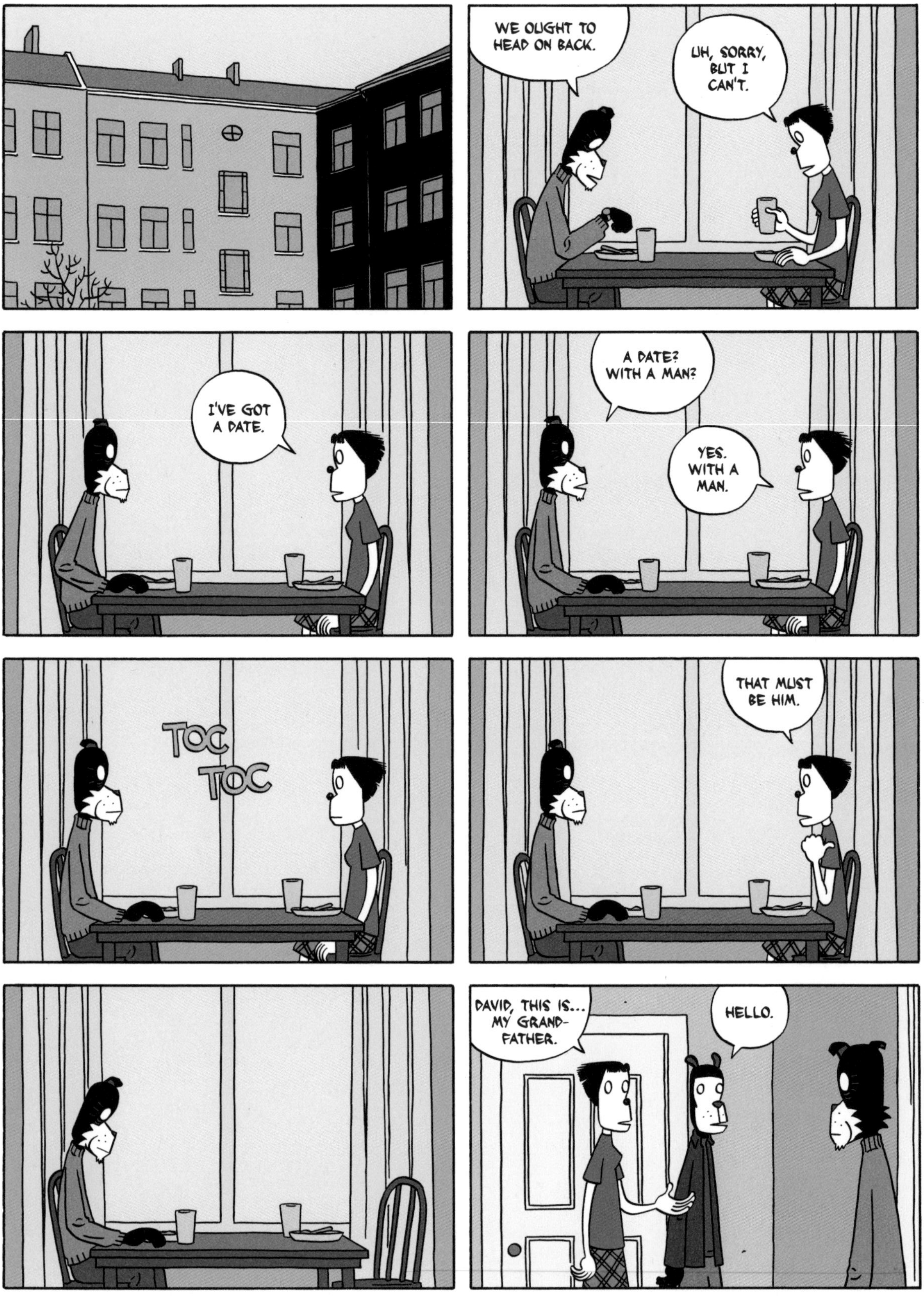
WE OUGHT TO HEAD ON BACK.
UH, SORRY, BUT I CAN'T.
I'VE GOT A DATE.
A DATE? WITH A MAN?
YES. WITH A MAN.
TOC TOC
THAT MUST BE HIM.
DAVID, THIS IS... MY GRAND-FATHER.
HELLO.

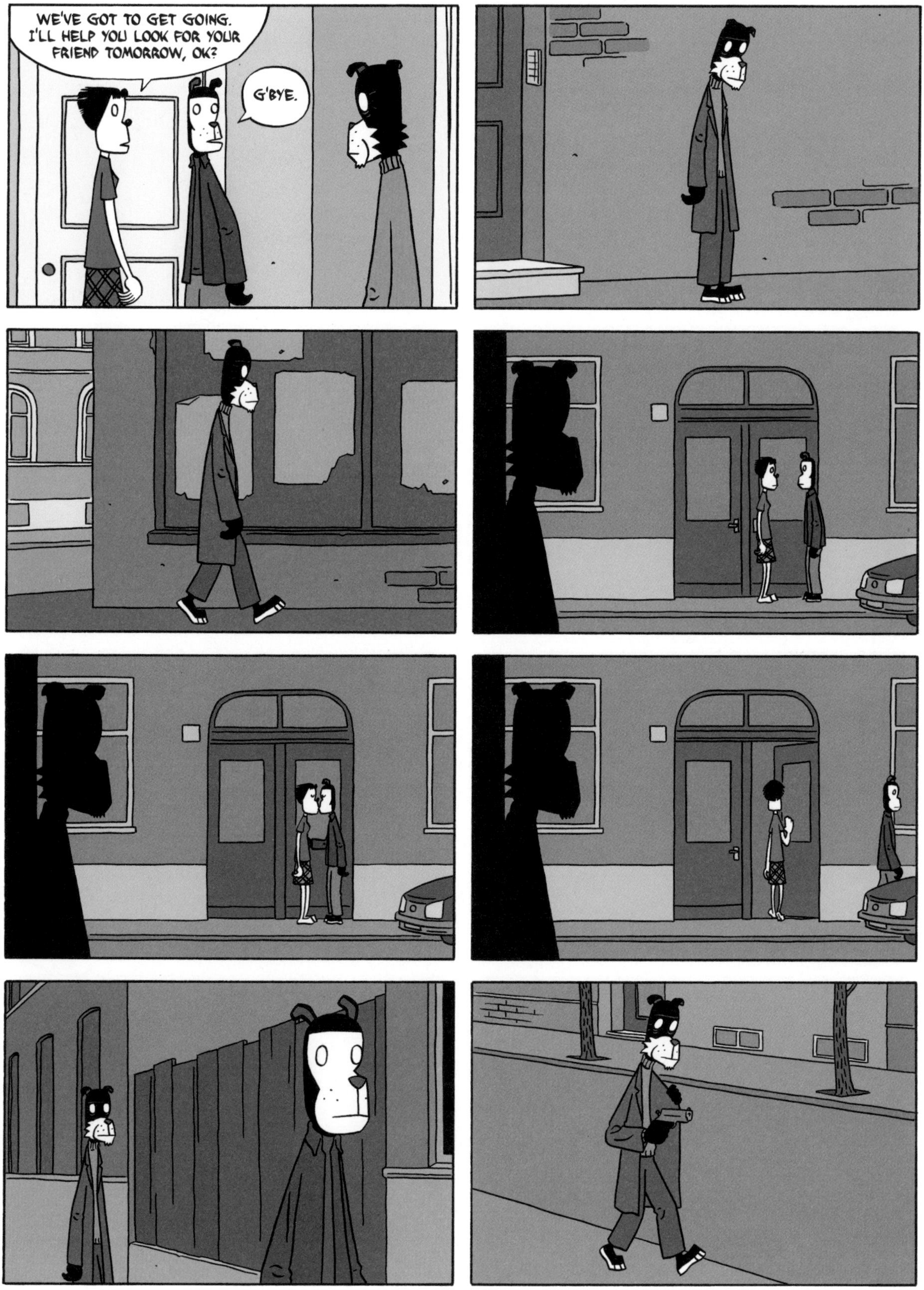
WE'VE GOT TO GET GOING. I'LL HELP YOU LOOK FOR YOUR FRIEND TOMORROW, OK?
G'BYE.

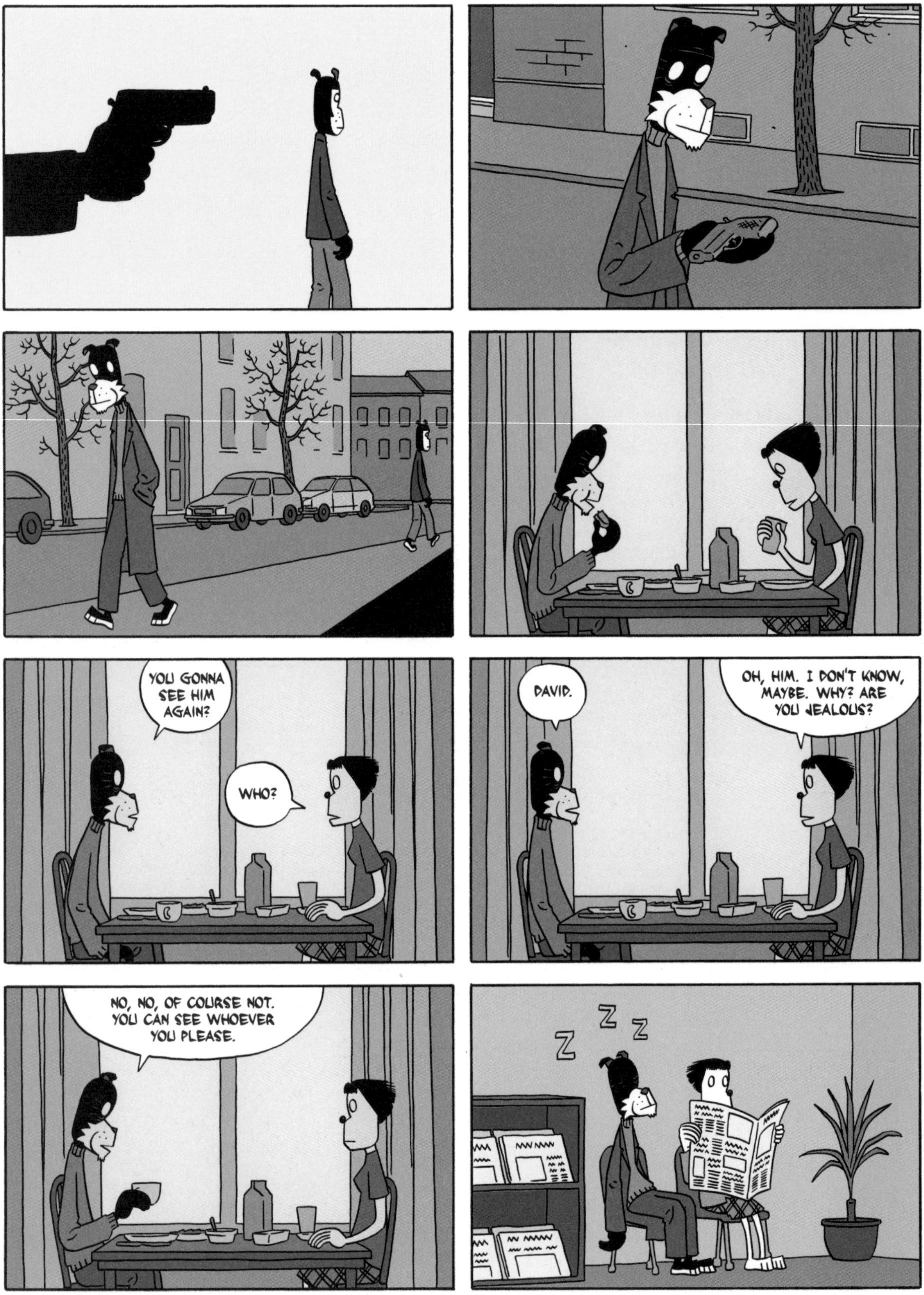
YOU GONNA SEE HIM AGAIN?
WHO?
DAVID.
OH, HIM. I DON'T KNOW, MAYBE. WHY? ARE YOU JEALOUS?
NO, NO, OF COURSE NOT. YOU CAN SEE WHOEVER YOU PLEASE.
Z Z Z

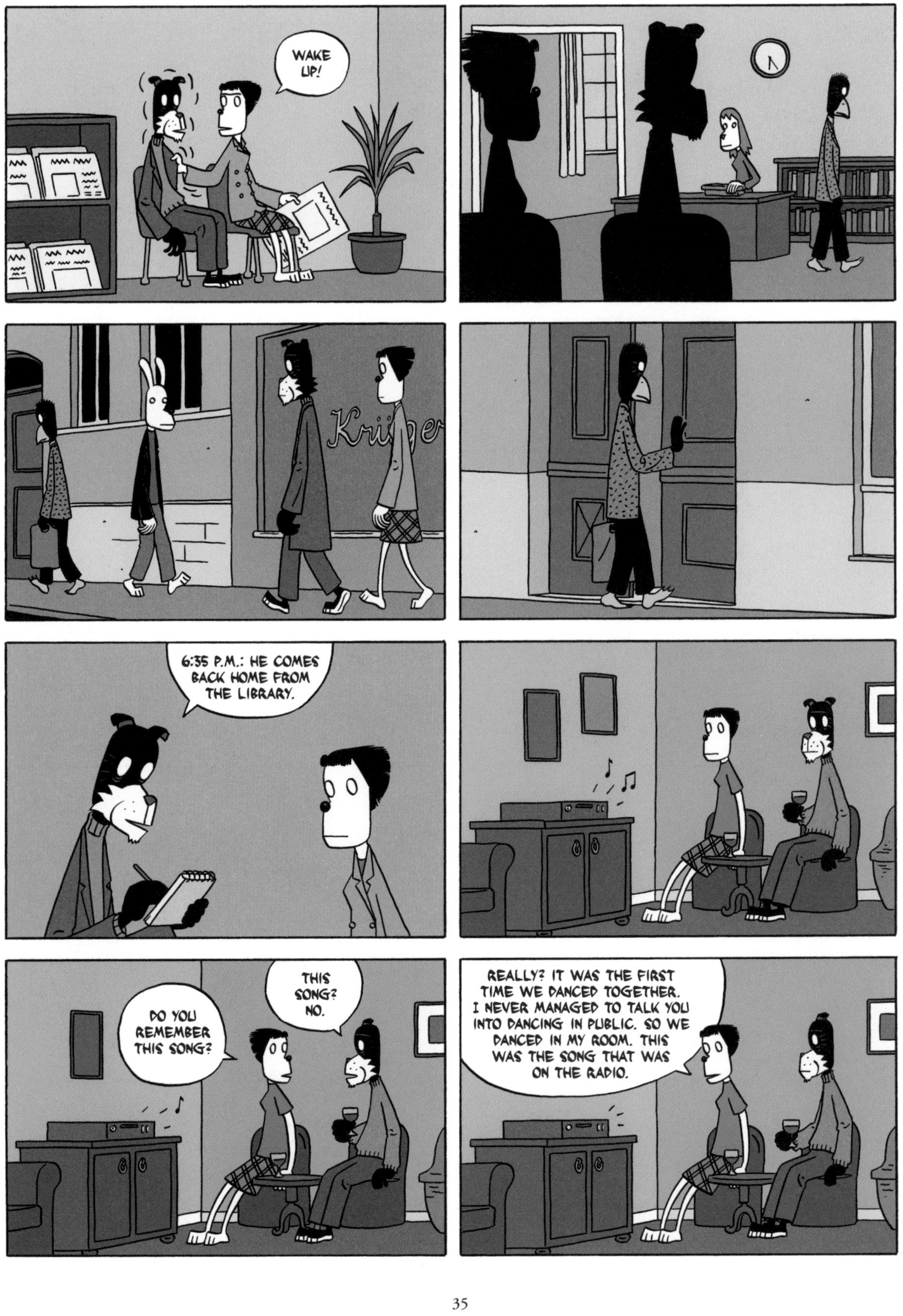
WAKE UP!
6:35 P.M.: HE COMES BACK HOME FROM THE LIBRARY.
DO YOU REMEMBER THIS SONG?
THIS SONG? NO.
REALLY? IT WAS THE FIRST TIME WE DANCED TOGETHER. I NEVER MANAGED TO TALK YOU INTO DANCING IN PUBLIC. SO WE DANCED IN MY ROOM. THIS WAS THE SONG THAT WAS ON THE RADIO.

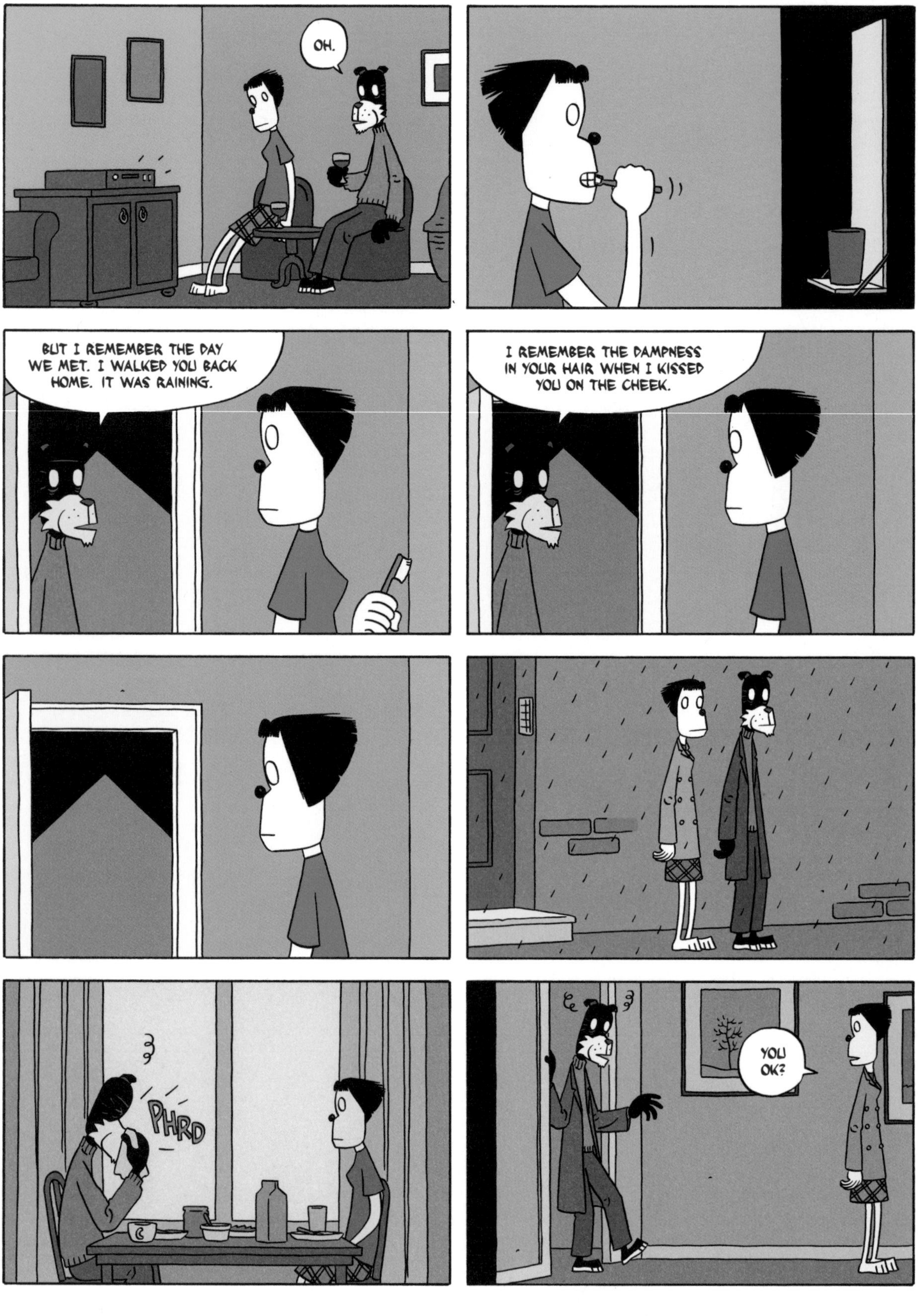
OH.
BUT I REMEMBER THE DAY WE MET. I WALKED YOU BACK HOME. IT WAS RAINING.
I REMEMBER THE DAMPNESS IN YOUR HAIR WHEN I KISSED YOU ON THE CHEEK.
PHRD
YOU OK?

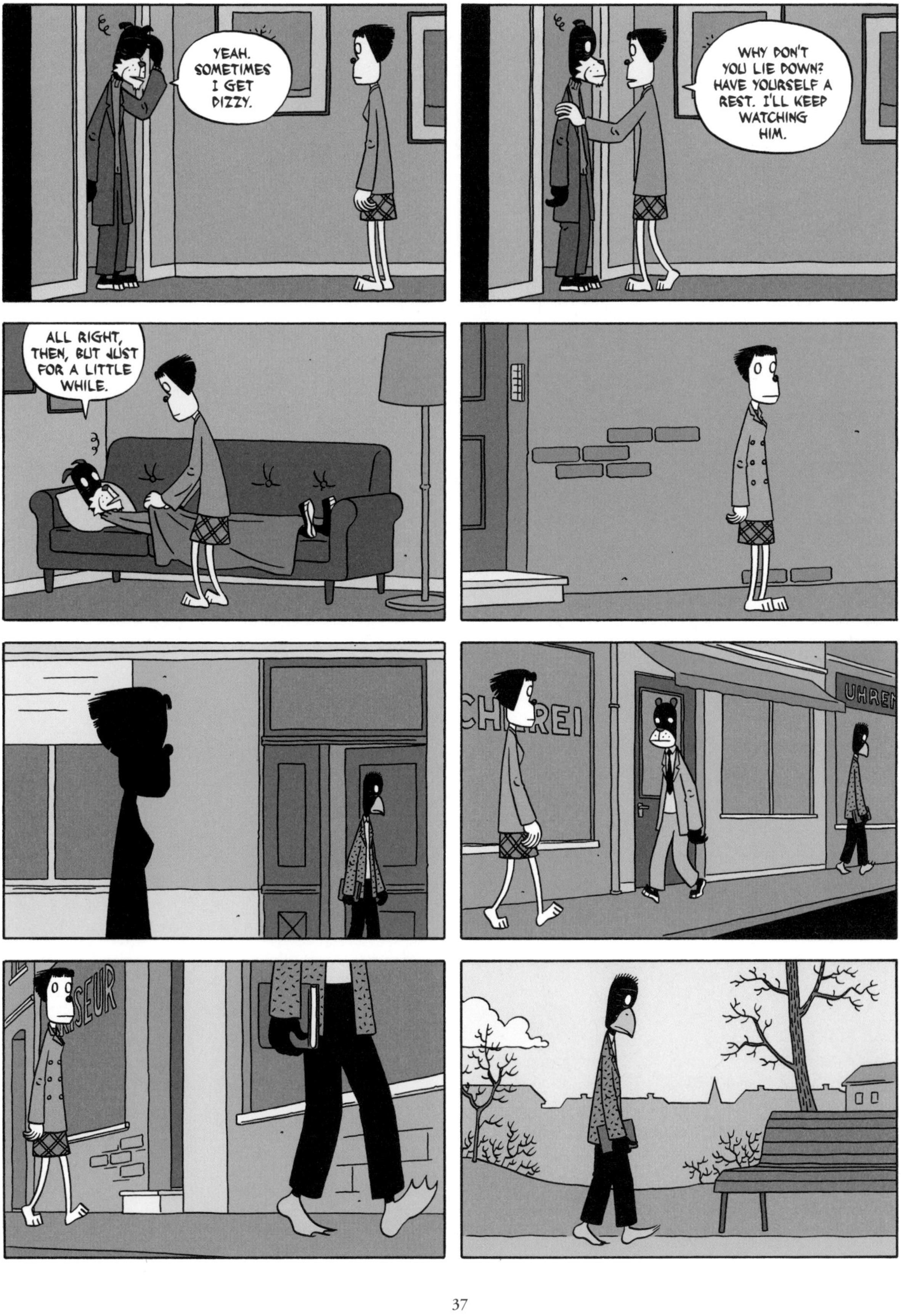
YEAH. SOMETIMES I GET DIZZY.
WHY DON'T YOU LIE DOWN? HAVE YOURSELF A REST. I'LL KEEP WATCHING HIM.
ALL RIGHT, THEN, BUT JUST FOR A LITTLE WHILE.

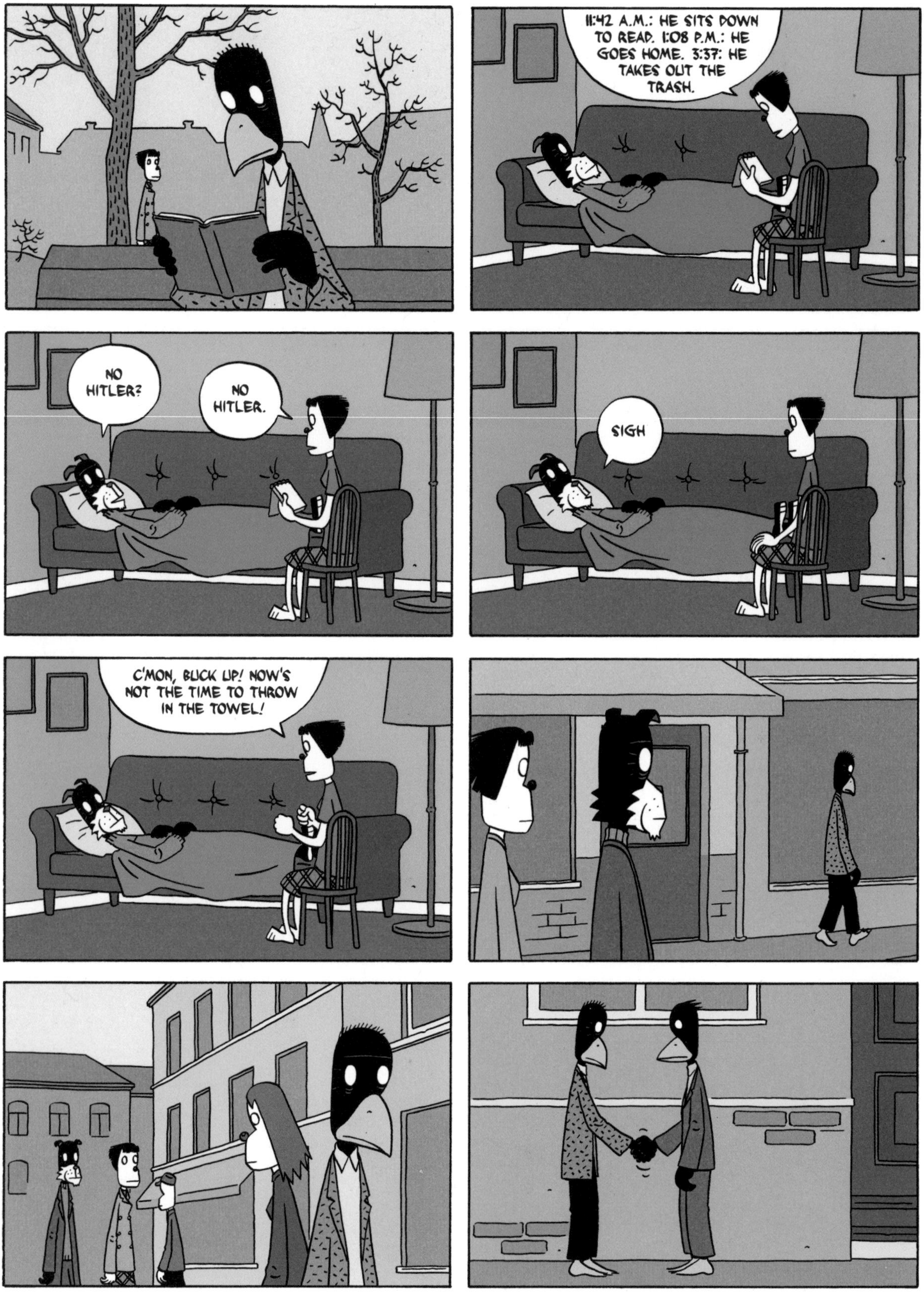
11:42 A.M.: HE SITS DOWN TO READ. 1:08 P.M.: HE GOES HOME. 3:37: HE TAKES OUT THE TRASH.
NO HITLER?
NO HITLER.
SIGH
C'MON, BUCK UP! NOW'S NOT THE TIME TO THROW IN THE TOWEL!

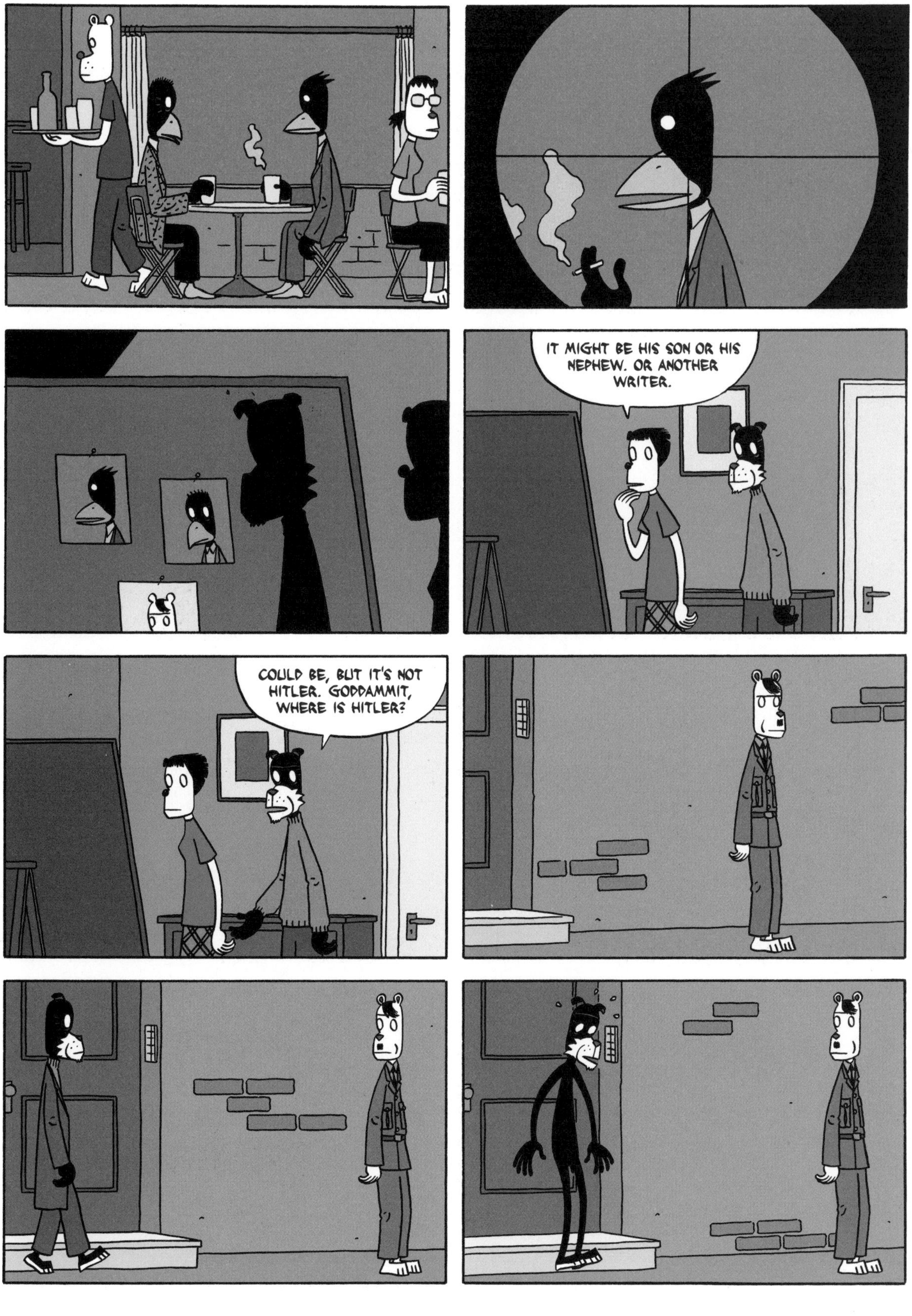
IT MIGHT BE HIS SON OR HIS NEPHEW. OR ANOTHER WRITER.
COULD BE, BUT IT'S NOT HITLER. GODDAMMIT, WHERE IS HITLER?

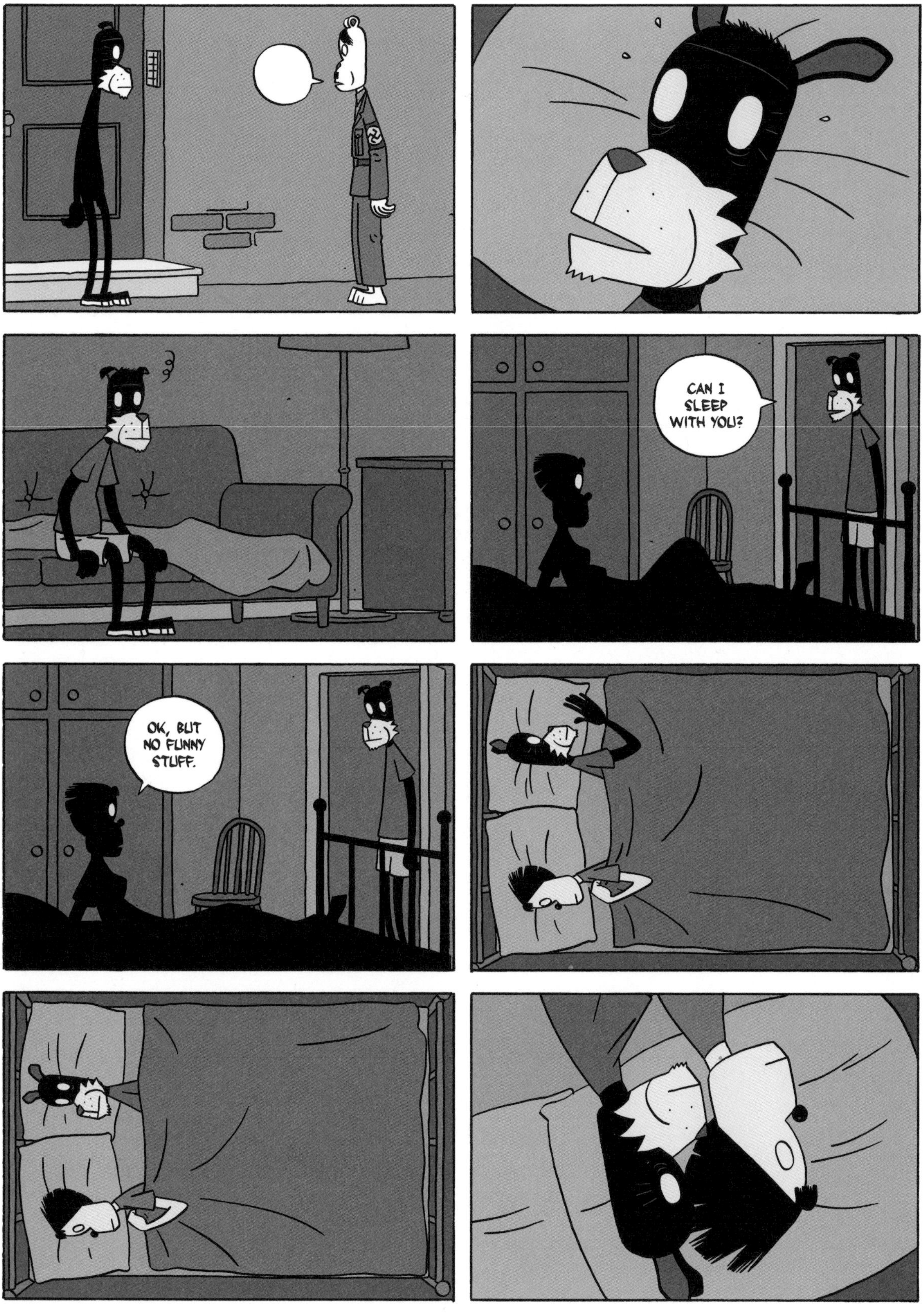
CAN I SLEEP WITH YOU?
OK, BUT NO FUNNY STUFF.

LOOKS LIKE IT'S GONNA BE A NICE DAY.

YES.

WHAT ARE WE DOING HERE? HE NEVER GOES OUT ON TUESDAYS.

LET'S GO.

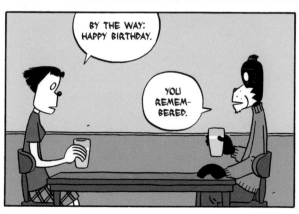
BY THE WAY: HAPPY BIRTHDAY.

YOU REMEMBERED.

WELL, AFTER ALL, WE DID CELEBRATE A BUNCH OF THEM TOGETHER. COME TO THINK OF IT, HOW OLD DOES THAT MAKE YOU?

OLD ENOUGH TO BE YOUR GRANDFATHER.

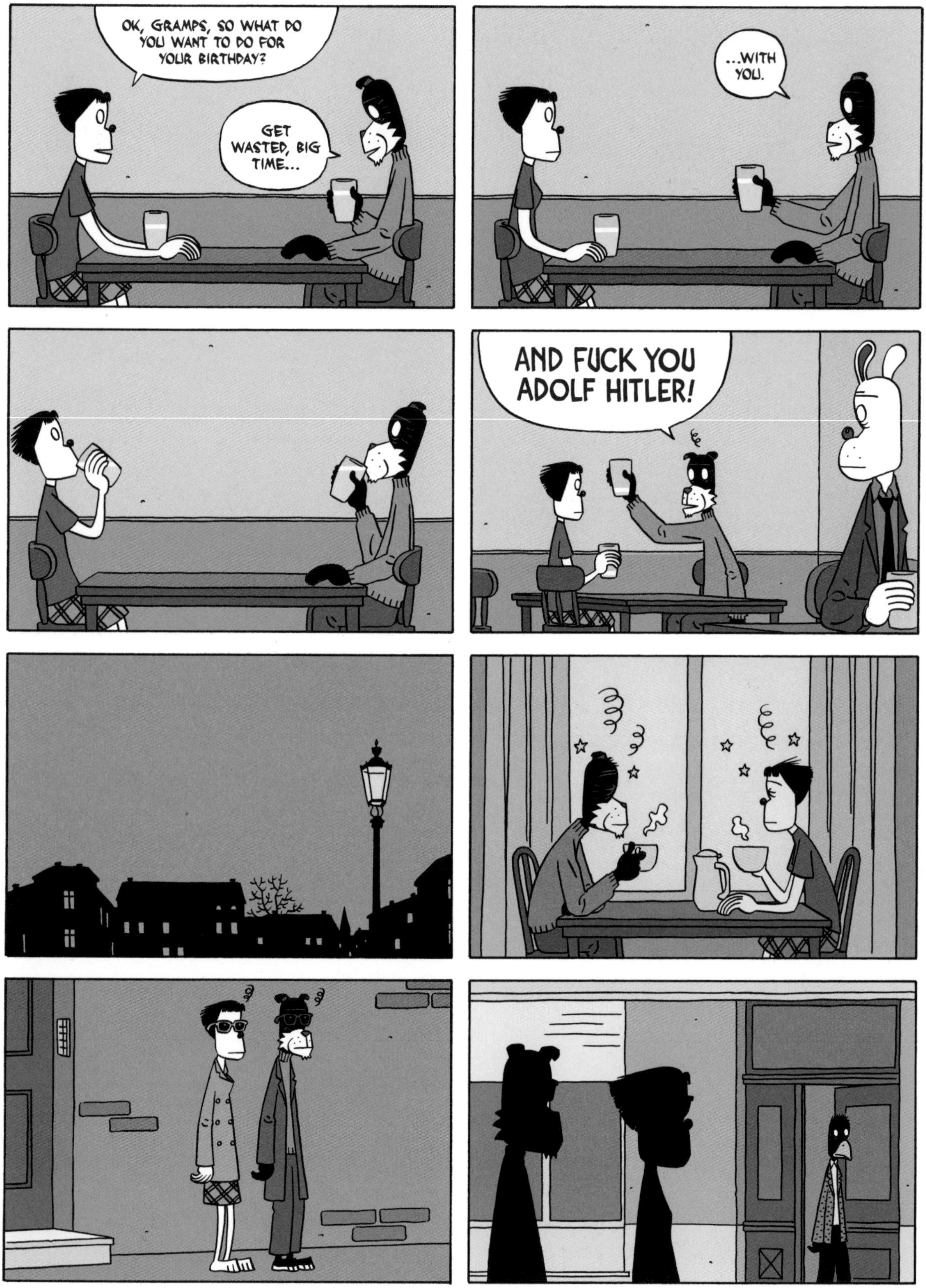
OK, GRAMPS, SO WHAT DO YOU WANT TO DO FOR YOUR BIRTHDAY?
GET WASTED, BIG TIME...
...WITH YOU.
AND FUCK YOU ADOLF HITLER!

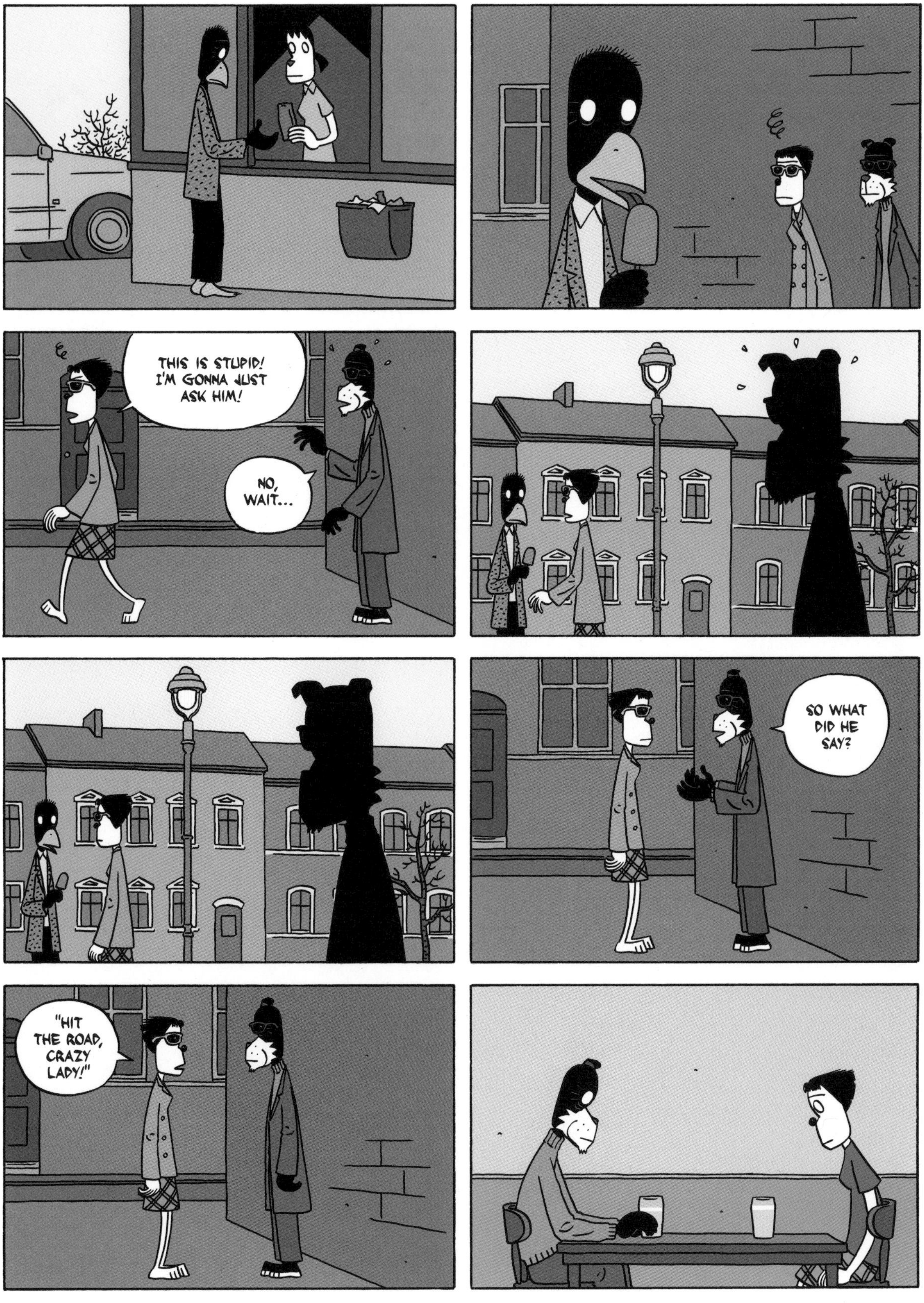
THIS IS STUPID! I'M GONNA JUST ASK HIM!
NO, WAIT...
SO WHAT DID HE SAY?
"HIT THE ROAD, CRAZY LADY!"

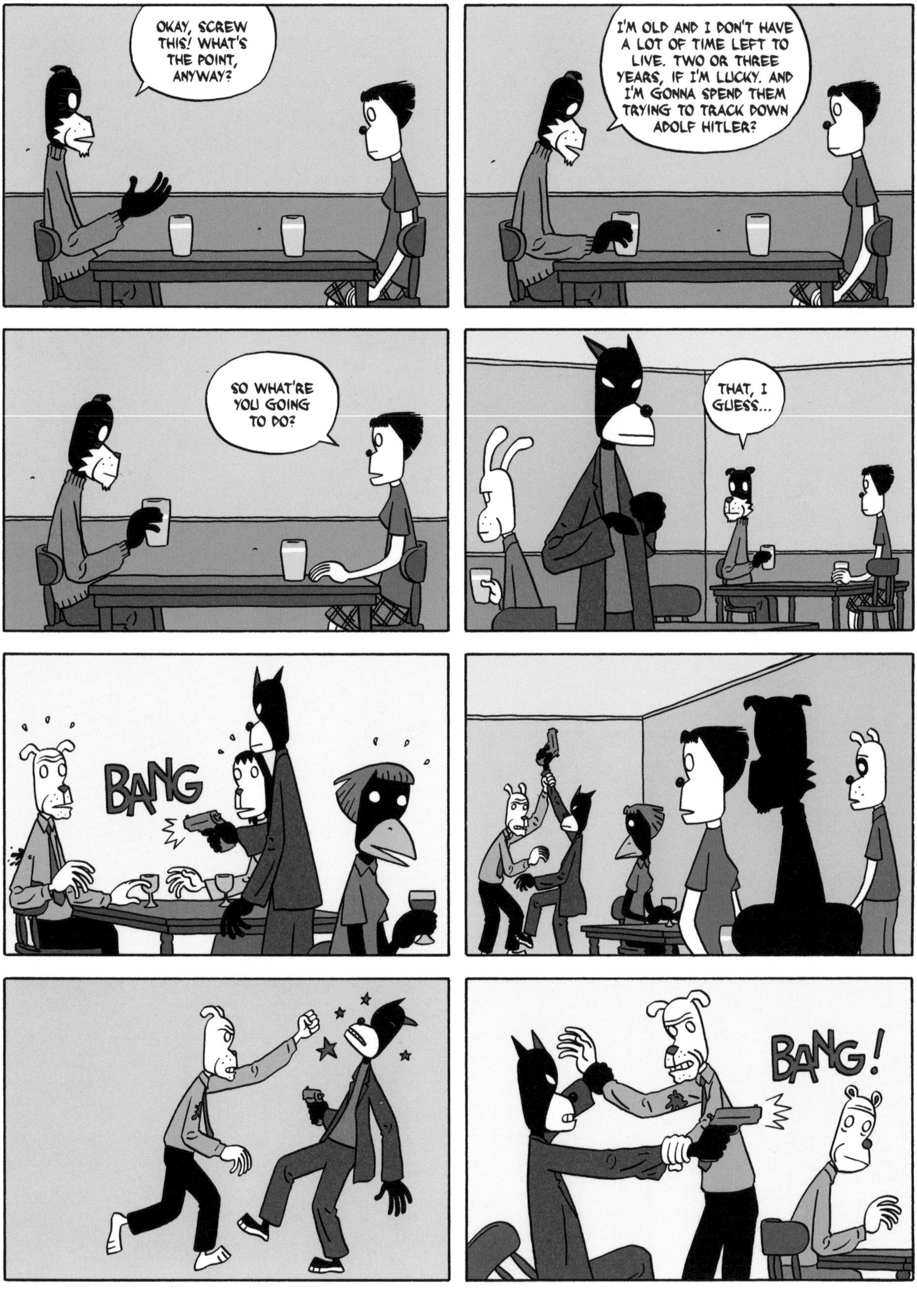
OKAY, SCREW THIS! WHAT'S THE POINT, ANYWAY?
I'M OLD AND I DON'T HAVE A LOT OF TIME LEFT TO LIVE. TWO OR THREE YEARS, IF I'M LUCKY. AND I'M GONNA SPEND THEM TRYING TO TRACK DOWN ADOLF HITLER?
SO WHAT'RE YOU GOING TO DO?
THAT, I GUESS...
BANG
BANG!

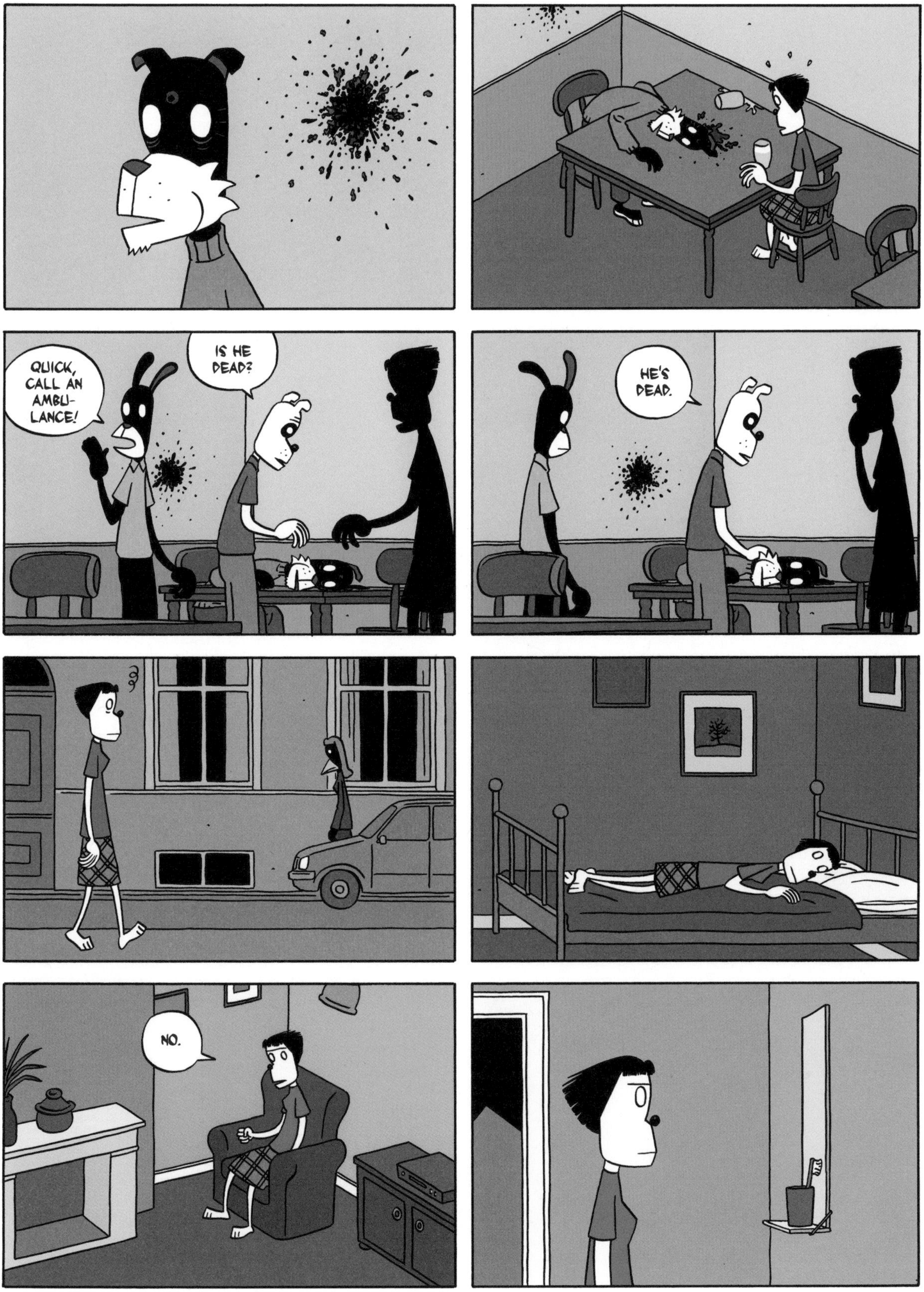
QUICK, CALL AN AMBU-LANCE!
IS HE DEAD?
HE'S DEAD.
NO.

FIFTY YEARS LATER...

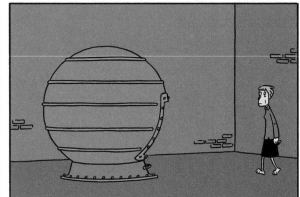

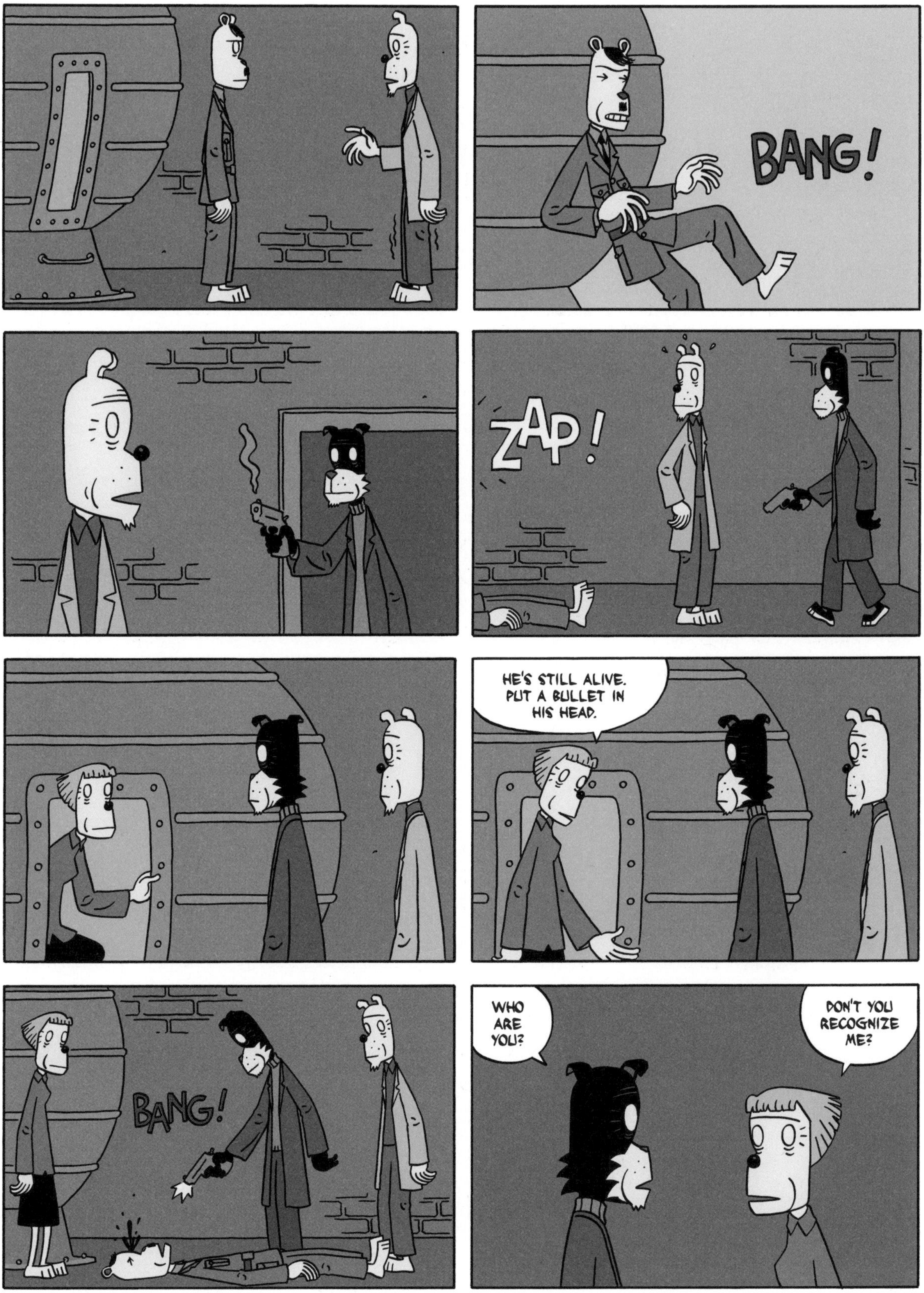
BANG!
ZAP!
HE'S STILL ALIVE. PUT A BULLET IN HIS HEAD.
BANG!
WHO ARE YOU?
DON'T YOU RECOGNIZE ME?

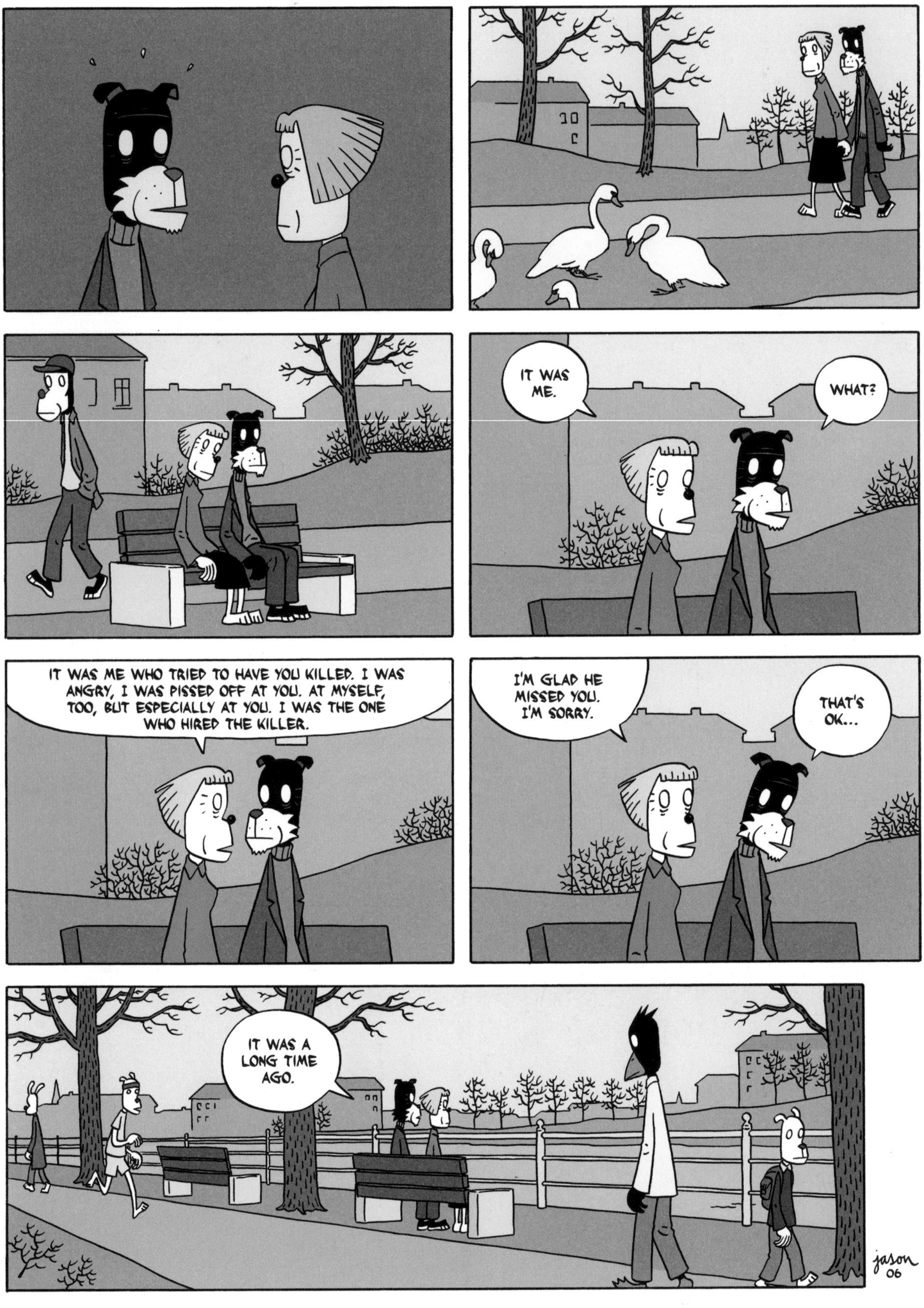
IT WAS ME.
WHAT?
IT WAS ME WHO TRIED TO HAVE YOU KILLED. I WAS ANGRY, I WAS PISSED OFF AT YOU. AT MYSELF, TOO, BUT ESPECIALLY AT YOU. I WAS THE ONE WHO HIRED THE KILLER.
I'M GLAD HE MISSED YOU. I'M SORRY.
THAT'S OK...
IT WAS A LONG TIME AGO.
jason 06